Cover Art:
MLC DESIGNS 4U

Publisher's Note:

This is a work of fiction. All names, characters, places, and events are the work of the author's imagination.

Any resemblance to real persons, places, or events is coincidental.

Solstice Publishing - www.solsticepublishing.com

The Quest

By Johnny Gunn

This book is dedicated to my lovely bride, Patty, in my full realization that it would never have come together without her trust and love.

Chapter One

The day is hot as only it can get in the Nevada desert, rolling waves of heat grabbing for what little air there might be at ground level, and remember what they say in all the tourist brochures, "It's a dry heat. No humidity. It feels good, this dry desert heat." Well, they can take their cute little brochures and put them somewhere equally hot, but definitely humid. Desert heat sucks the life right out of you if you don't fight it every second. Water, water, and more water, and then find some shade regularly. Of course, finding shade in the desert is about as easy as winning the lottery twice. A cold beer never hurt anytime. If I said water, water, more water, I can say beer, beer, and more beer can't I?

I grew up in the humid hot south, humidity so thick I don't ever remember wearing a dry shirt as a kid. We got out of there when I was ten-years-old and moved west, Montana west, and Montana has about the best weather in the world. Unless you don't like snow this deep, cold this cold, and winds this strong. Now, I'm deep in the Great Basin, deep in Nevada's driest desert area. I wish I could do my work in Maui or San Francisco, or Puerto Vallarta.

I'm not really a scientist, but I am an amateur archeologist and I truly love the desert; the wide-open vistas filled with history can keep me occupied for days. The color in the desert is what catches one off guard. Pinks and grays blending in with blues and greens, and all soft pastel in form. Clouds can soar into thunderstorms, roiling so high they seem to reach outer space, and one can always find camels and elephants, pterodactyls and whales soaring about the ether if one just sits with a touch of patience. The wide-open desert is a fine place to just sit, contemplate one's purpose, one's reason for being, one's possible goal if there is such a thing. I always have believed in such things as purpose, reason, goals, and the desert has made many of my days into opportunities for such mind meanderings. Today is one of those days, with undulating waves of heat clamoring for its place in my being.

My specialty, if you can call it that, is the history of the ancient civilizations that existed in the deserts of the Great Basin, that area that fills in the map between the Rocky Mountains and the Sierra Nevada. The intriguing part of those hunter-gatherers was what they left for us, their writing on rocks that we call petroglyphs and rock art. Historians tell us through various types of dating that most of these writings began following the last glaciated period, which would put their start date somewhere between eight thousand years and ten thousand years ago. 'What was life like then?', I ask myself so often, and to a degree I wish I could go back and find out. That's where I am right now, letting my mind go in reverse, wondering what it would have been like thousands of years ago if I were standing on this exact spot. Which am I, a writer or a slacker? I can spend hours and days sitting in the desert, then taking notes, then eventually converting those notes into something that an editor might think of as being comprehensible. I am unquestionably in the best profession in the world.

I have my camp set up along a very small stream in the foothills above the Silver Peak playa in central west Nevada. It's a beautiful little camp with fresh water, firewood, and a breeze in the evening to make life worth living after a day on the playa. The mountains dawdle right down to the playa, ever so gently, maybe five miles from camp and that's where I've been, following the base of the mountains along the western edge of the playa for several days. I really should do this work in the winter, but not me, not strong willed, Tom Henry. Let's do it in July or August or maybe even June or September, you know when it's really hot. Later, back at camp I would get the laptop out and put my notes into some kind of order. Finally, it would be time to drink some cold beer, burn a steak over hot coals, maybe even crisp up some potatoes.

I was following a series of rock scratchings, and as I moved from one group of petroglyphs to the next, I had the feeling I wasn't alone. This isn't a new feeling, but I looked around anyway, just to make sure, but like always, I never actually saw anyone or anything. The feeling just wouldn't go away, and I finally sat down on a protruding rock shelf to relax and have another drink from my canteen. This is the great Nevada desert, and if you ask a city dude, you'd be told 'why go there? There's nothing there,' they'd say, 'just sand and rock.' Well, city dudes should spend more time in the desert and less time on asphalt if they really want to know about life.

I'm surrounded by life, just as those souls thousands of years ago were, the ones responsible for these petroglyphs. A couple of horned toads are sitting on rocks nearby, as well as a couple of little lizards doing their push-ups. Canyon wrens are gently whistling to me, telling me I am in their back yard, not to make a mess. The lizards are so funny to watch, but in truth, their push-ups are a defensive mechanism. Their eyes are such that their own movement allows them to see potential danger.

Overhead, two ravens, clowns of the ether, caroused their way through thin air, calling, laughing, making jest in the raven's way. Still, there was something I couldn't see. I could feel it, something making my skin crawl, sending those little electronic shocks up and down my spine.

"Make yourself known," I said loudly and, of course, nothing happened. That was really brilliant, Tom. Wouldn't you have a cat if someone answered that little call of helplessness?

I hope I'm not alone in thinking that it's okay to talk to oneself when out alone like this. I always talk to myself, give myself hell sometimes, ask questions to keep

7

my mind working, discuss what the hell I'm doing. I have to keep some kind of perspective or I'll go nuts. Look at me, I'm almost 35-years-old, big old receding hairline, no paunch though. I wouldn't say lovely to look at, but accepted as a writer of archeology and things historic, and I'm wandering around the desert talking to myself about the possibility of ghosts or something. I rather doubt my mother or anyone else in the family would want to try to understand. I did try to explain once and that was a complete disaster. "Tom," I remember my father saying, "You have an advanced degree in history with a minor in journalism. I doubt your peers spend so much time talking to themselves as they work on an article or a piece of history." It was said with love, though, so I just smiled and asked myself another question.

Finally, the feelings of someone being nearby were just too strong to ignore so I gave it up and headed back to my truck. It was time for a cold beer and a couple of hours in a cool and shady place, like a comfortable saloon. The little mining town of Silver Peak was a few miles back on a sand and gravel road, and as I jumped and crow hopped my way off the hillside, tripping through the rocks and brush, a great trembling came over me. I actually felt an energy field building, and anxiety turned to fright, the beginnings of terror.

Have you ever been about to fall and you can't stop yourself? Have you seen a car wreck develop and you are helpless to stop it, even though you are one of the drivers? My soul crawled with fear on the one hand and I was overwhelmed by a desire to get the hell out of there. I was not alone, I was in grave danger, and yet I was alone, and there was no obvious danger. Imagine what it would have been like thousands of years ago, and my heart beats faster, my blood gets as heavy as bunker oil, my feet won't do as told, and I know I'm in very deep trouble.

I've been in the middle of severe desert thunderstorms, been close enough to a blast of lightning to be knocked on my ass and have my beard singed. That's what I was feeling, the building of a massive bolt of lightning, screaming thunder, the angry voice of all the gods of all time, but there were no clouds, only hot air, sand, hot limestone rocks, and fear. The sand was hotter than it should have been, burning through expensive hiking boots, and the air was starting to swirl. There are levels of panic, I think, anxiety on up to screaming fright, and I was climbing the scale. My head swiveled from side to side, my mind shouted, 'look there! No, over there!' I stormed off that hillside not caring if I fell, just wanting desperately to get back to the truck.

I actually ran when I got to level ground, and that's when I saw him, an old man in a wool poncho wearing a South American style peasant's hat, the ones with ear flaps and high peaks. Hotter than hell and this old guy is wearing a wool shirt, and his baggy pants made from scraps of whatever, tied at the waist with a rope, a scene made for comedy if I hadn't been so screwed up in my head.

He was an ancient one, possibly Mayan, possibly Aztec, history etched in his bronze face, his eyes were bright, alert, spread wide from a beaked nose. He was slight of build, not actually skinny, but certainly not carrying any extra ballast. His hands didn't show they spent hours working, rather they were soft, not callused, nails clean and trimmed. Although I had the feeling he was ancient in years, he wasn't bent over or even out of breath. His animal skin mocs kicked up little swirls of dust as he marched toward me. He wasn't shuffling along, he really was marching, hearing a drummer, fife playing loudly, and he was coming straight for me. His hands were thin, with long fine fingers, the hands and fingers one might find on an artist or musician. He was just yards from my truck and yet when I was on the hillside I never saw him. This isn't right, and I'm standing here with a mostly empty canteen, a rock hammer, and nothing else with which to protect myself. Protect myself? Where did that come from?

The apparition walked right up to me and I couldn't move, couldn't run away, just stood waiting for him.

"You have no one with you?" he commented as we came face to face. Everything about him told me he was from south of the border, as we say, but he had no accent. In fact, his English was well spoken. He sounded as one might think a literate and learned man might sound.

"No, old man, I'm here alone. You're a long way from town, did you walk?" I was incredulous that an old man would be several miles in the desert in this heat and on foot. "It has to be well over a hundred degrees, old man. Are you okay?"

"Your name is Tom," he said, ignoring my question. Was his a question? Or was he making a statement? Or was my imagination out of control? I've never seen this person before, ever, and yet he comes out of the desert dust, alone for all the world to see, and calls me by name. All I could do was answer him.

"That's right. Tom Henry. What's yours?" I could feel pricks of panic, panic that told me to run for my life, but I couldn't. I tried to remember that this was just an old man, maybe a prospector. I knew instinctively he wasn't. So, I didn't run away, I couldn't, I simply answered his question, stuck out my hand to say hello.

"We are here to meet, Tom. Let's go over there, to that rock overhang, and sit in the shade. There is much to discuss and time is rather short."

My writer/scientist self said to stay and listen, while the rest of me was screaming, "Run, Tom, run!" Is this who I felt was watching me? He walked out here and knew where to find me? I didn't run, I walked over to the little cave with the old man, settled down onto the cool sand, and felt wave after wave of energy flow through my body, etching my soul, coming from marrow deep inside and moving to the surface, and then reversing itself. One second, I boiled, the next shivered from cold, one minute terror filled, the next calm, almost mellow. The urge to flee was equaled by a desire to know what was happening.

I was overwhelmed and on the verge of passing out, but the old man brought me out of the reverie. "On this little planet we call Earth, are many of these zones of influence where it is possible for us to move from one plane to another. There was a time when all humans understood this, but being arrogant and selfish, not willing to accept or understand that you are not alone, you have lost those opportunities. From time to time, it's necessary for us to establish communications with your subspecies in order to maintain our galactic control."

What the hell is he talking about? Why is he talking to me? I must look as befuddled as I feel and I find that I'm really paying attention to the old guy. I should just get up and walk away, run away, but I can't. He's talking about how the original people so long ago had ways of moving between various realities. I've read so many stories about shamans being able to move between here and there, never really understanding, and he's talking about that. I can't run. I can't even stand up, I'm so engrossed.

Also, Tom, think just a minute. He said, "maintain galactic control." What on Earth is he talking about? How would an apparition from thousands of years ago, and that's what I have to believe he is, have anything to say about galactic control? The first thoughts of heat stroke are also coming to the surface in my muddled mind, but -- galactic control? -- that is one I can't understand.

All my adult life I've wanted this experience, to talk with an ancient. We can't even decipher their rock etching and I'm sitting with one. There were times during my less than stellar attempts at higher education when I believed this was possible, and it was hammered home that there are no such things as travel between planes of existence, that there are no "old people" walking around. Now I'm sitting in the shade, whacked out by sunstroke or actually talking with an ancient.

Make your mind pay attention, Tom; this is why you're out here. Pay attention, big boy, because you will have to write this and you know it. Get all the facts locked in that pea brain of yours and remember everything this ancient piece of history is saying to you. I have an old trick that works when I need to calm myself, but pretending to grip a baseball for a hard tight slider wasn't working. Nothing was working, but I was still intently listening at least.

"During the time we are together, human Tom, you will learn things only a few of your species know about. You may experience some fright as I come and go, but not enough to do any major damage, and even so, there isn't anything you could do about it anyway." There was no smile as he said this, and the fright was palpable. Was that a threat? Said with a smile, I would have responded in kind, but what he said was as close to intimidation as I want to get right now.

I must be calming down because what I'm thinking is, *you have a lot of nerve scaring the hell out of me and then threatening me on top of that? Be careful old man, if you make a move on me I will knock the hell out of your old head. He knows me? He says he has to maintain galactic control? What the hell does subspecies mean? And that crack about not being able to do anything about it anyway, was that supposed to be a joke or a threat?*

"I understand all the questions racing through your uncontrolled mind, and many of those questions will be answered. What's important right now is that you try to put order to your thoughts as you listen to mine. Worlds, time, ideas, galactic and universal order, even the answer to the question of creation, will become very clear to you during our time together. There is nothing to fear, and when all is completed, you will be in the same condition, physically and mentally, as you are now."

I had just been lectured, and wasn't sure I appreciated some of his comments, and that one about my mental state really got me. But then again, what to do about it? I was still anxious, but not terrified, and I wanted to know more from this old man who talked about galactic control, about answers to our creation. He sat there looking perplexed, and again told me to put my mind in order. Put my mind in order? Could I even begin to explain what is happening? I can't comprehend what is happening and he wants me to put my mind in order. My head hurts.

With a long and slender forefinger he drew a circle in the sand, drew lines to separate the circle into three parts, and when finished, I was looking at what could pass for the peace symbol so popular back in the 1960s. "Each part of this symbol represents a part of us: you, me, and all the other subspecies of the universe." He stabbed a long finger into the sand. "This is the present. Where we are now. This over here," and he jabbed again, "is the past, where we were, and this," he drove his finger deep into the sand this time, "is the future, where we will be.

"To move from one plane to another is simply a matter of transporting from an energy field or zone, using the knowledge of the universe. These things are of extreme importance, human Tom, don't neglect to learn what I'm teaching. When you come to a zone, such as the one we're in now, you must establish contact with those who control the door by showing the sign," and he pointed at his circle in the sand. "Make the mark of where you wish to go, that is, before, or to come. The mark of two crossed lines represents before, while a series of three dots or points indicates to come. To be, in other words, where we are now, is indicated by your letter 'V'.

13

"Don't forget any of this, human Tom. Our voyages will sometimes separate us and you will need to travel without me." Then he was gone, simply gone. I had a raging headache pulsing across my forehead, behind my eyes, almost making me physically ill. That lunch break of a bowl of rice and beans was churning closer and closer to escape and I had to put considerable thought and energy into keeping it in place. It took most of what strength I had left to drag myself to my truck. I found my canteen and took a long pull of hot desert water. I remembered a bottle of hooch I had hidden under the seat, and even though it was just as hot as the sand I was standing in, I took a mighty draught. That wasn't smart, I thought, now along with heat stroke or whatever, I'm bombed, too.

What on Earth is going on? Too much heat is the first thought, and I jumped in the truck for the five-mile ride into town for some cold water, and most important, cold beer. I kept looking in the rear view mirror. For what? Did I expect to see an old Aztec loping along behind the pickup? In my state of mind, it would not have surprised me. Reality was slowly replacing uncontrolled anxiety, and I came to accept that I had had a visit with an ancient, someone who understood the ways of the shamans and the legends of the old people. Even if all this is heat stroke, I sure as hell will never forget what that old man was trying to tell me.

I believe there are various planes of existence, despite the fact that college professors refuse to allow that kind of thinking in their classrooms. Every ancient culture on earth has stories about traveling between these planes, about their gods moving about through different existences, about how the bad and the good are moved about to places like what we call heaven or hell. And, I am willing to believe right this minute that I just had a meeting, a coming together with a being that is fully capable of moving from

14

one plane of existence to another. I also realize I have just totally lost contact with reality.

The bar was filled with miners and truck drivers, mill workers and heavy equipment operators, so I didn't dare try to tell the story of what had just happened. I'd still be the laughing stock of Silver Peak, and so I just tucked the episode away in my memory. Right now, I was ready for that beer.

"You sure look like hell, Rock Man. You find some ghosts out there in the desert?" Old Hard Rock Sam Mason laughed loud and strong, and was joined by most of the other men in the bar. He had a name for everyone, usually something to do with mining, but for me, since I chase petroglyphs, he just calls me Rock Man and he'll never know just how close to the truth he had come. "Come on, Rock Man, what the hell did you see? You're white as one of those rock artist ghosts you always look for."

"Just the heat, Sam. Just the heat." There is not enough cold beer in the world to get me to tell these guys what I just went through. What did I just go through? I can't tell myself right now. "Too much sun, Sam. Too much sun. How about a cold brew, Alice? I need it today." I can't even bring myself to flirt or give a big come-on to Alice, one of the few single ladies in Silver Peak. A few cold ones later I was still asking myself, what the hell just happened? When I got back to camp, my mind had settled a little bit and I determined to make myself understand what happened to me. I was surprised to see the bottoms of my boots when I changed into moccasins. Strong hiking boots that cost way too much money were blistered on the soles. That can't be right, but it was. Those rocks had to have been well over 300 degrees to cause that kind of damage. Was the Aztec, as I started calling him, responsible for this?

I lit the fire and got ready to burn the corn flakes as my mind tried to put things in order. He said, "Our voyages will sometimes separate us." Voyages? The thought of being able to talk with an ancient still swirls, but I can feel danger all around me. I actually did burn the corn flakes, in this case chicken thighs over an open flame as I tried and tried to put some kind of logic to what had happened. I've read about men lost at sea who turn up years later with tales of strange men and beasts taking them in, caring for them, sending them home again, but this is different.

Maybe it was sunstroke, and then again, maybe none of this happened. Maybe I'm simply losing my mind. It didn't take long for me to convince myself that I needed to go home, go back to my little apartment in Virginia City and put it all together, get the hell out of the sun for a couple of weeks. The only thing I'm sure of, I will not be discussing this little episode with anyone. On the other hand, it might not be a bad idea to look up the descriptions of some of those nomadic hunter-gatherer tribes that moved through this area following the last glaciated period. Could that be what I met, an ancient from 8,000 years ago?

It took most of the morning to pack up my camp but I had made up my mind as I crawled into my sleeping bag the night before that I had to drive out to the site of the little rock overhang before that hard, hot four-hour drive back to Virginia City. I'm fully hydrated, I've had a good night's sleep and a strong cup of coffee, so if anything is really wrong, I should know it.

The only footprints in the area of the cave were mine. No one but me had been here yesterday and now I have to accept the fact that I was suffering from delusions of some kind. But, what about that old man's comments of universal councils, about subspecies, and voyages? More, what about the threats, or at least perceived threats that I heard from him? Yes, I heard them, I talked with him, I saw him. There are no footprints, Tom. Go home, go back to Virginia City and get some rest.

16

The little cave was just as I remembered it. *Well of course it is you fool. It's just an overhang of rock, only goes back about three feet, not high enough for someone to stand up.* I sat down in the shade and just contemplated again what that old man had said. I'm big and strong, still pretty damn fit, and I have to admit I was afraid of that little guy. My mind is going off somewhere that I don't like. Everything tells me right now, there was no old man, there was no conversation, there were no threats, and now that I'm hydrated I should understand that. I don't understand that at all.

I found myself looking in the rear view mirror often, always asking myself as facetiously as possible, *do you see an old Aztec back there?* I never saw him, but I looked often.

I'd been gone for several weeks on this excursion so the mail had stacked up, the e-mail even deeper and no matter how much time and effort I put into recreating a normal life, pictures of that old man stayed in my head. Sitting under the rock overhang and hearing him talk about galactic this and universal that, telling me I'm going on voyages with him, and drawing pictures in the sand simply added to my desire to know this old man better. He is an ancient one, I'm sure, but that would make him a ghost, and I don't think I want to believe in ghosts. I've never been more confused in my life and still I don't dare attempt to start a conversation with someone about my desert encounter.

Chapter Two

It was almost a year ago. It's so difficult to keep time straight now that time has no meaning after that old man invaded my life, changed the way I think about everything. Has it really been a year or just a day? Or is it that time has an enlarged meaning? Time and space are one. Distance is meaningless. Yesterday could be tomorrow and today simply represents now, which is where I am, now, with an old Aztec friend sitting on the edge of my bed.

Why did I just describe him as friend? I'm terrified of this creature and he doesn't fit my desired description of friend. I'm positive he threatened me that day near Silver Peak and yet I'm almost glad to see him, to welcome him to my home. If he really is one of the old people, here is an opportunity to learn things that few today would know: to understand the rock art, to discover how the wise ones, the shamans could move between planes of existence, to follow an historical thread from those that pecked on rocks to today's Native Americans. My god, he has so much to offer yet I'm still afraid of him.

It's been a year since I met the old one: Riba, time traveler, inter-dimensional traveler, sage of the ages, tormentor of my soul. He and those around him tested my mental strength, tested it to a breaking point, and now, as usual, with no forewarning of his arrival, he's standing before me. "Riba. Old friend, Riba. I thought we had parted company. To what am I honored by your presence?" I loved to tease the guy, not too much because his powers could destroy me, but enough to catch his attention. I remember actually making the guy smile, almost laugh, once. He just stood there at the foot of my bed, cool as all hell, skin just as iridescent as I remembered, shaking his ancient head at me. Sometimes that old head would shake

18

in rebuke, and sometimes in lack of understanding of the human spirit.

The big point here is, did I really almost make him smile once? I just said that but I can't for the life of me remember when I might have done that. What is this creature doing to me? We met once in the desert and there sure as hell wasn't any smiling going on that day. All the fear and terror are returning, and yet he has implanted some kind of memories that I don't understand at all. I feel I've been with him more than just that once, yet I'm sure I haven't. I just said to myself that I love to tease this old fraud, but I've never done that. "What have you done to me, Riba?" And, now that I think of it, how do I even know that your name is Riba?

"These are all implanted memories aren't they? You want something from me and you think the only way you'll get it is to terrorize me. You're wrong. You can't frighten me, Riba. I won't tell you anything. Anything! This is more than just a con, this is an attempt to control me through mind implants, through brain washing. I won't allow you to use me for whatever nefarious scheme you have in mind. You represent evil, Riba, not the old people, not the ancients that delighted themselves with rock art and petroglyphs. Stay away from me."

"You humans can't control your thoughts any more now than you did when we first made contact with you, human Tom, and that was almost two million of your years ago. Why can't you put your mind in order?"

"I thought your last visit was to be our only time together." My voice was scratchy as I said this, not full of anger as I wished it to be. I'm flat out scared of this old man.

"Those who came before and will come again, have need of your services, human Tom. I'm sorry if I caused you pain, but it's important we again go to the place of coming, the place where we first met. I can't explain further.   Only Qadroth can talk about what is needed, and so you must venture to our place."

Riba was always condescending when he spoke of human evolution. I was never sure exactly why, but he said our minds evolved differently from those in other galaxies, and weren't as advanced as so many other life forms. It hurt when he talked this way, but I learned over time, he didn't say these things with intent to hurt, it was just his way.   He always knew what I was thinking, sometimes, I think, even before I did.

How is it I know all this? I've had one encounter with this demon and I feel I've been with him dozens of times.   This is impossible.   Those same old worries are returning.   I can't remember all of what Riba has said we did. What's worse, did he really say anything? I feel as if I have been with him, held discussions, carried on conversations, went places, and yet I know we, I, have not. He says that we have been together before, that we have done things together, and I feel we have, yet I don't know what.   I simply know we have, and don't have a clue as to what we did, where we went, to whom we talked. Was I on other planets?   If we had a venture last year, I can't remember for sure, and yet I'm willing to tell myself we did. He obviously has control of my mind.

The memories are a mist, a fog, as if I can see the lighthouse only because I know it's there. He said Qadroth, I know I've heard the name, but I can't recall who this person is, or why I can remember the name.   Fears of madness fill my mind as this apparition I call Riba continues to intimidate. I'm willing to join with him in whatever he has in mind. If we can travel through time, backwards and forwards, I want to visit these wonderful people from several thousand years ago that chipped pictures in rocks, told stories we can't decipher today, and bring the people of our age a history of which we aren't aware. Eight thousand years ago is a long time and those people, human in every respect, must be very different from anyone I could possibly know. Are their rock pictures a language that can be learned? What a wonderful thought that is. I want answers to these kinds of questions and I feel right now, only Riba can give me those answers. I must stay with him, must learn from him, even if he continues to work so hard at humiliating me and the rest of my race.

He wants to return to the place we first met, the place where I was introduced to the universe. Our place. "Yes, Riba. We'll go." I gave my thought voice, and I could see in his squinty little violet eyes he was pleased. Dancing eyes is a description that is lacking in spirit when it refers to Riba. When he is pleased those eyes bore into my soul and when he's upset, which is often, the eyes narrow down, turn flint gray, and eat right through my soul. I want him to know I'm angry at the way he has invaded my life, at the way he simply makes statements that he assumes I will obey, and I can't put voice to my anger. I'm angry with you, Riba, I think but can't say. He knows it, though, because his eyes just flicked over at me and they were flat gray.

Our place, deep in the Nevada desert, just south of the mining community of Silver Peak, a place where locals have talked about ghosts and spirits, talked about strange feelings of energy along mountain paths, is a place of spiritual strength and power. Our place along the western edge of the Silver Peak playa, nestled up against the first croppings of hills that reach up from the virtually flat pan, is the place where thousands of years ago, people etched pictures into the rocks. We speak of prehistoric activities and I have an opportunity to be in their time, to meet, talk with, and understand what the rocks are saying. I've written about these people and their lives, about the country they lived in and the food they grubbed for, and because of this little man who says he is a time and space traveler, I

21

am going to meet them. Yes, I say to myself, yes, let's go to our place.

That's where we'll be going, to the place I first met Riba, where I first learned of intellectual travel, where I first discovered that we are not alone on this planet, in this galaxy, in this universe, and most importantly, the place where I discovered that past, present and future, at times, can be one. Inter-dimensional is a concept that is not often discussed over a martini or two after work. In fact, one can drive one's friends into the next room trying to open a conversation about the subject. "Time travel? Without a vehicle? Maybe it's the sun, Tom. Take a rest, buddy."

I'm not sure that I haven't lost my mind, I don't know where these thoughts are coming from, I would never attempt to tell anyone about Riba, or about our first meeting. I'm remembering things that I know for a fact never happened, I know things I've never learned, and this old man is a threat. I have to remember that above all else. I've been terrified to discuss the things I've learned, or in some way know about, for fear of being put in a white coat in which my arms are no longer usable, my hands bound behind my back, where attendants terrorize the patients. Am I mad? There are times I believe it, regardless of the fact those around me insist I'm not. I still fear being awakened some morning by way of an electric cattle prod wielded by an overweight madam in a white uniform, drooling in her eagerness to hurt me.

I've tried not to think of Riba or the Universal Council for more than a year, put all thoughts out of my mind, and now, a rush of memories. I cannot remember why I know about the Universal Council. Did Riba tell me? Have I met with them? There are those who believe madness has a way of going and coming. I fear I may not have control of my mind any longer. I fear that.

"It's good for you to remember our first time together, human Tom, for you will need to remember much of what I taught. Let your mind go back to our first few meetings, so this meeting will be prosperous." Riba always, always knew what I was thinking. "I dwell in your mind, I therefore know your mind. You see, my body principal, I am a part of you, even when you see me outside your body." It took a long time getting used to being called human Tom or body principal.

Memories are flooding my mind, but are they mine? Is Riba planting thoughts, ideas, memories that may not really exist? He just said our first few meetings, and yet there was only that one. If these memories are real, and I do feel anxious, more terror than anxiety, then why haven't I thought about any of our so-called exploits before, during the year Riba hasn't been with me? Those thoughts are dominant right now. I must be careful, must not let myself be drawn into something that is illegal or simply wrong. Riba is not a kind person, and whatever his agenda might be he is doing everything possible to make me a part of it. I'm positive I've seen him just once, yet when he talks about various ventures I know, I think I know what he's talking about.

I was terrified when I first came to understand that I was more than me, that my self, ego-self, intuitive-self, one-self, was not one, but was host to Riba and could host others as well. My first encounter with Riba was not conducive to further encounters, and yet, over time, I actually feel close to the old guy. Time. It has so many different meanings to me now. What time is it in which Riba and I dwell? Reality is a concept, isn't it? We say reality, and we mean here and now. We mean we think we know where we are and what we're doing, but reality; it's just a concept. If that is the case then what is space? Is there such a thing or is the many concepts of reality simply space, and what would time be? No, no, Tom, you will make yourself utterly mad if you let your mind play these tricks.

Here and now may actually be simply where you are at this moment. I've been 'here,' meaning the twenty first century on the planet Earth in the galaxy we call the Milky Way, and in the blink of an eye, been 'here,' in quite another galaxy, on quite another planet, in quite another time, and all of it 'reality' in my mind.

Riba just chuckles when I try to put the pieces together. "Your mind is totally out of control, human Tom. Accept what you see, what you feel. We move through the planes of time and distance because we can." He was never able to tell me how this is done, and as we apparently became friends, I simply accepted him for what he appears to be. I look on him as a friend, sometimes, as someone to be feared, at times, and as a form of madness on my part, as well.

Chapter Three

Memory bank overload, visions of problems swirling about me; foggy, but real. All the memories from that first visit come flooding back, the heat from the rocks, the old Aztec just walking right up to me, I could feel that first experience, happening as it did while I was in the middle of something I enjoyed. Maybe that's the way life hands us problems, gets us feeling good about something, then dumps on us. I had been walking along the edge of the Silver Peak Playa, looking for petroglyphs, rock writing from prehistoric times. I kept a log on topo maps, backed those up with photographs, and often had my findings published in archeological journals around the world. Sometimes the nature of an article would find its way into travel magazines and wire service copy as well. It's a good living I always told myself. When no one was watching, I would then roll my eyes because it's a way out for me.

I'm one of those people that can procrastinate my way out of morning coffee if I'm not careful so traveling the western states, camping more often than staying in a motel, simply enjoying where I am is a very pleasant lifestyle. For someone to pay me to do this is the best thing ever. To send me notes suggesting other areas and other ancient peoples is thick chocolate frosting on double chocolate cake. Now, this old Aztec, or whatever the hell he is, wants to take me back to Silver Peak and there is that possibility that I might get to meet with some of the old people. What kind of a dream am I living? This simply can't be true, but it seems to be. There is always a down side to something that sounds as good as what I'm thinking of right now.

This entity scares that hell out of me. I have memories of things I've never done and he did that. He has threatened me and made little nasty comments about the

human species.   What else is he capable of?   The red lights
are flashing and the klaxon is blaring.

This area was very wet, tropical in nature, at the end
of the last glaciated period, and the playa is the leavings of
a vast prehistoric lake, teeming with fish, waterfowl, and
other game.   The surrounding mountains drained into the
lake and offered shelter, food, and firewood.   It was natural
for the nomadic tribes that wandered the high ground of
what we call the Great Basin today to either make this a
home place, or at the least a stop over, and the rock pecking
probably carries tremendous historical data if anyone ever
figures out what the 'glyphs mean.   I have always believed
that my own small endeavors might help in the matter.

There have been both scholarly tomes and some
best described as other than scholarly written about
petroglyphs and rock art, and there are people that believe
they are able to read some of the etchings.   Most of those
that study the period believe that petroglyphs predate the
rock art.   Petroglyphs are etched into rock faces while rock
art is just that: artistically painted onto rocks with primitive
paints.   How much time between those that etched and
those that painted is simply unknown although some have
tried to use various dating techniques to find an answer.
The meaning of the messages, however, is unknown.

In some places there are hundreds, even thousands
of individual petroglyphs, such as newspaper rock in
Arizona,   and   in   other   places,   just   a   few   along   a
mountainside such as those I was contemplating near Silver
Peak, deep in the great basin, deep in the desert known as
Nevada.

Ancient   people   around   the   world   pecked   their
stories into rocks, in Egypt, France, Spain, to mention a
few, and of course, in North, South, and Central America.
Histories of older tribes talk about traveling between
realities.   In Arizona and New Mexico many original
people used Kivas and such near what might be called

zones of extreme energy, and shamans often used evil and good from other realities in their religious teaching. Is Riba a shaman? Or is he an evil entity from another realm?

Funny isn't it, that when we find something ancient, the first thing we do is say it had some religious significance to the old people? What will happen several thousand years from now when an advanced culture finds some of our automobiles in a landfill? Will they be considered religious objects? What about the twelve billion baby diapers? I'd enjoy reading that educated paper. We won't go into finding discarded cell phones, but it is thoughts like these that make my work so interesting. Friends tell me I spend too much time alone in the desert, that I have addled my puny little mind with the effort, but I don't pay much attention. I like myself and my work enough that being alone, but so much a part of the old people, that I don't feel bad about my time in this pursuit.

Those people lived with their environment, not as we fight our environment today. Everything they did had a meaning in their lives, the way their shelters were built, where and how they hunted, and probably most important knowing what could harm them or make them ill. This was a closeness mostly unknown today and leads me to believe that the petroglyphs had to have a serious meaning to others coming upon them.

Each age of human development offers vast changes from the previous age and what I'm finding with these rock histories are well developed minds that felt it was important to leave some form of communication for others like them. Were these writings messages of where to find streams filled with fish, where to find a good supply of firewood, where to find adequate caves in which to live for a period of time? Or, as our libraries are filled, are these deep philosophical thoughts, written in picture form, thoughts detailing gods, morals, living testimony to life immediately following glaciers and trouble?

27

Whoever the souls were, they had to have been convinced that the writing served a purpose because petroglyphs are found throughout the world, with many here in the Great Basin. These in the Silver Peak Playa date back between eight and ten thousand years. Think about sitting for hours on end with a stone in your hand, pecking away at a larger stone, creating a picture of a big horn sheep or a deer. It took hours of monotonous effort for each little piece and my mind is saying these old people had to have a purpose in their work. Will I discover what that purpose is by following along with whatever Riba has planned? I really want to believe.

Are the ghosts of those old people still watching over the area? Sometimes a mystical feeling fills my own soul, like someone watching, or often, I'll feel a force field gathering, generating these thoughts, little needles of pricking awareness all over my body, running up and down my spine, giving me the jitters. Anxiety, not fear, is what I tell myself when this happens, but also, I expect to see an ancient standing near his writing effort, guarding it, offering it for posterity. Seeing an ancient, rock in hand pecking at stone hasn't happened to me, but possibly it has to others in the area.

When the Sixteen-To-One mine was operating and the haul trucks were moving ore from the mine, down a five mile gravel road to the mill, just west of where I was that day I first met my universal teacher, many of the drivers on the late shift talked about seeing lights, sometimes shadows of what they described as men moving near the roadway. Some said they really did see people moving across the road, walking through the sage. When the area was observed during daylight, there would never be any footprints, except for those left by the desert critters scampering about.

Were the drivers just tired? Or were these men who had been told too many stories? Our imaginations are powerful, there's no doubt, but for a story to be told, it must have started somewhere, had at least a modicum of truth.   How did these stories get started?   Many of the Native American tribes and nations have tales about a parallel world.   Sometimes that world is peopled by evil creatures, sometimes by kind and generous deities, sometimes by a combination of both, and most of the legends have particular points of geography where transport between the worlds takes place. Was I working in one of those mystical areas?   Was that why I could feel surges of energy from time to time?   Or, more likely, was I spending too much time in the desert, under the hot sun, as many of my friends supposed?

In the great southwest, including the Great Basin, some of these sacred and powerful points are believed to be guarded by Yeti.   For many followers of the spirit world, Yeti and Bigfoot are one and the same. I was never sure in my own mind whether to believe any of those tales of supernatural existence.   Never sure that is until that first meeting with Riba. I refer to that time of my life as BR. That is, Before Riba.   That first time is etched in my mind, and this is the first time the story has been told, the first time I've felt confident enough in my own memory to put it to paper. Just moments ago, I questioned whether any of this actually happened, and now, I seem to remember all of it as if it was yesterday.   Does Riba control my mind as well as reside there?

During the first meeting, nothing of what I just described was actually said, but rather, implanted. I seem to know about time and space, about then and now, and am quite willing to accept the fact that there is a Universal Council, and that Riba can travel about through the heavens as he wishes. I questioned my sanity when we met, and now again, this apparition has made himself present and I'm still questioning my sanity.

It was when our family moved to Montana that I became so involved in history. In the south, history is hundreds of years old, that is the history of Europeans in North America, but in Montana, history is not even 200-years-old. What the old timers told a tow-headed 10-year-old inflamed a mind that hasn't stopped its investigations to this day. I was not quite a teenager when I had my first history piece published in a little weekly newspaper, and I was hooked for life. And, now; Riba. My god, what is it that is really happening?

He spoke of another journey, but it's one I can't remember. Or does he consider that first meeting a journey? Riba gives me that dirty look of his, the one he uses when he thinks my human mind is out of control.

"It's time for our journey to begin, human Tom. Forgive me for bringing you pain, but since I'm now residing in your mind, the only way to come forth is through a slight amount of pain to you. Remember for all time, my name is Riba. Just say the name and I'll come to you. It doesn't matter what part of universal time I'm in, or for that matter, where I'll come to you, I'll understand immediately that you have called for me.

"Sit now, facing me, rest your hands on your thighs and we will become one. We'll be in a different place in a moment."

There was no swirling of clouds or visions fading in and out as we so often find in movies and television but he wasn't kidding. In a blink we had passed from my little apartment high in the Virginia Range of Northern Nevada, in the old mining town of Virginia City, we had traveled two hundred fifty miles, and I was sitting in the sand in front of the that little cave in the desert, south of Silver Peak. There must have been a massive thunderstorm going on for I was getting soaked, water cascading over my head. Riba of course was standing inside the cave, dry and amused.

"Come inside, human Tom. Come in out of the water." He walked down into the cavern, deep under the rocks.

"I don't remember this part of the cave, Riba. We had gone to a small little rock overhang before. This isn't the same place." He just shook his head at me, but he was smiling. Old Riba could smile after all. Etch this one in my brain, old man.

"I understand your confusion, human Tom. Yes, this is the same little cavern, but some eight thousand years before our first visit. That wasn't a thunderstorm getting you wet my friend, it was a waterfall." I took his smile to mean two things, he was enjoying watching me get soaked to the bone, and he took pleasure in making me feel foolish one more time.

"What you're seeing now is the whole cavern, and where we were was the cavern filled in by the sands of time," Riba continued.

I'm actually here in the time of the ancients. Will I get to meet them? Damn, Riba don't just walk off like that, this is my dream. It was dark in the cave, but I could see well enough to keep up with the little guy. His shuffle step carried him at a pretty good clip as he led me deeper into the cave.

"Riba, wait. This is the time of the petroglyphs, don't walk away now, we need to talk. I need some answers." He just kept walking as if he hadn't heard a word I'd said. "Damn, Riba, please." Nothing.

As we moved around an outcropping of rock, we came into a well-lit grotto, lighted not by torches as I expected, but generated from small glowing bulbs floating about the interior of the cave. They didn't seem to be attached to anything, but gave more than adequate light.

As my eyes adjusted, I found we were in a room full of people dressed in fine brocade robes covering what appeared to be lightweight silk shirts and pantaloons. All were wearing warm, well-made fur covered boots, and

31

none wore hats or headpieces. I had in my mind we would be meeting the residents of that cave, indigenous natives, possibly even savage in appearance and instead these are well-dressed, well-groomed men. I was suddenly more confused than ever before in my life as the room itself transformed into a nicely furnished, well-lit meeting room. It would meet the description of conference room in any convention brochure. The same lighting was provided and there were about fifteen people seated around on a circular divan looking at me and Riba. I don't know what has just happened but I do know I'm not in the company of those that populated that desert cave eight thousand years before my birth. I'm not going to find any answers to the petroglyph mysteries from these people.

A tall, elegantly robed man with flowing silver white hair and bright blue eyes rose to greet us. "Riba and human Tom. I'm glad you're here, we've been expecting you. Please, come in and join us. Human Tom, I am Qadroth, one of those responsible for your existence as a subspecies." His voice was deep and resonant, and as he spoke to us I could almost see life sparkle in his eyes while at the same time, he was very formal, slightly distant in his manner yes, but a friendly sort of person. Once again, as with Riba, there was no indication of any kind of accent.

If we were in a cave, eight thousand years before my birth, how is it these people are speaking English, a language unknown until thousands of years later? I was in awe on the one hand, intrigued, but also fearful of what might happen. Not quite terror, but I was fearful. If these people are related to Riba it probably means I'm not going to get the answers to this intrigue. They know my name, speak my language, and knew we were coming, even knew when, apparently.

The old man's skin was all colors. All colors. Light pink, as human Europeans, yellowish as Asians, very deep brown to black as Africans, and every shade of brown as the rest of the world, and all at the same time. Amazing, yet not distracting either. Qadroth, as he called himself, literally glowed, and when I looked over at Riba, his outward appearance was the same. Riba is a changeling?

It came to me at about that time that we were all dressed similarly. I was not in jeans and cowboy shirt but in a comfortable silk feeling shirt with a vest of very soft, maybe kid-skin soft, leather with a wonderful fur collar. I was wearing pantaloons and fur lined boots. I come to their cave; I'm dressed as they are. I pulled a sleeve up just a bit, but my skin has not taken on the tones of Qadroth's. Try as I might I could not come up with a single thought to answer any of the questions flooding my sunstroked mind.

After all these years of studying different aspects of human evolution, my mind has snapped. I'm going to be a quivering mass at the end of the mental ward hallway and evil and ugly men in white uniforms will beat me daily to make me better. I must be strong and make myself understand that none of this is happening.

"Riba, I see the human mind hasn't evolved one single molecule since we implanted the seed so long ago."

"No, Qadroth, I'm afraid you're right. Their capacity to fill their minds with thousands of thoughts and never ever sorting them into use and non-use categories is a wonder. How they have survived with this mind clutter is something we should study more in depth.

"Your invitation indicated an urgency, Qadroth. How can we serve your Imperial Mind? Human Tom and I are at your service."

Well, now, Riba, my friend, you're taking a bit for granted aren't you? 'Human Tom and I are at your service?' I don't seem to recall a discussion along these lines.

I don't think I want to get into the habit of just accepting that I have been drafted into someone's service by people and organizations I've never even heard of.

"Riba, let's step back for just a moment and look at this picture. I don't mean to be rude in any way, Qadroth, Riba, but where I come from, people ask. Ask me if I want to serve you and when you ask, outline what it is that will be expected of me." That's only fair, I think. I'm not being unkind or rude or discourteous, but I'm making sure that I'm looking out for good old number one here.

"Right now, you have the upper hand because I don't know where I am, I don't know any of you, and I have no idea what you are talking about. It may well be that I will want to work with you, but right now I don't have those thoughts at all. In fact, I would feel far more comfortable if you just sent me home." I was looking around the room finding many faces looking back at me, but without much indication whether or not they agreed with me or were going to put a spear through me and put me on the fire for snacks a little later. Why did I think spear? I guess because I was really hoping that I would be moving into a cave filled with those that lived on earth eight thousand years ago. Fascinating how life can change on one that fast.

Qadroth spoke before Riba could get a word out. "Human Tom, this is my fault entirely. It is I who have been rude, even discourteous, not you."

This will take a long time to understand. I didn't say the words rude and discourteous out loud. I said them in my mind. They understand every single thing I'm thinking.

The boss of the meeting continued, "Within the galaxies that make up the Universal Council we all have each other's thoughts and ideas, we all know each other and the problems each of us face. I should have had a meeting with you and Riba alone and explained what our problem is, and yes, asked if you would help not arbitrarily indicate that you will help. I apologize, human Tom. Listen to what we have to say, listen to this horrible problem that has come our way, and consider this an invitation to join with us in finding solutions."

That's better. This is something I can live with, and I will listen to their dilemma, and if I can, I will help. This is diplomacy at an extreme level and this person Qadroth is very adept at manipulating, at getting his way. Something to remember, Tom, something to stash in the back of the memory bank.

We settled onto that great and comfortable circled divan and I have to say I was feeling much better about the whole thing. Everyone's attention was directed toward the obvious leader, Qadroth. In the center of the circle was a slightly sunken fire pit, glowing with embers and offering considerable warmth to the room, despite marble flooring and hard walls. Even though I couldn't control this feeling that I have gone quite bonkers, I was genuinely enjoying what was happening, taking in all I was seeing and feeling.

"Human Tom, please let your mind rest." Qadroth, speaking plainly, but not severely, was trying to hold me in check. "Everything will be answered, and I can assure you, you have not 'gone bonkers' as you quaintly phrased it. I have called this meeting of the Universal Council because of a serious threat to our existence."

There it is. The Universal Council that Riba and this man have spoken of, and I'm sitting in the middle of it. Whatever the hell 'it' is.

"Each of you here represents a different subspecies in our universe. Human Tom, from the galaxy we call Marq, Sarcathian Tene, from the outer galaxy Dosen-II, Quarian Riba, from our home galaxy Tanso, and so on.

"To make sure we all understand what's happening, we must review our history. Human Tom, this will all be new to you because the earth humans would never allow themselves to become a part of our council, our grand scheme, this happening millions of years before your time. When the Quarian tribes first became aware of the fact we could mind travel to any point in the universe, millions of years ago, as you count, but a blink of our eye, we set forth to populate the universe, and found within many of the galaxies existing life forms that we could successfully mate with.

"The most successful, of course, are our dear friends, the Sarcathians, and the least successful and most difficult, I might add, were those we call humans from the galaxy, Marq. When their minds evolved from the simple fur covered, large but gentle animals we mated with into a human, it was frightful. For the first several thousand generations or so, this evolvement was slow in coming, but then, it just overpowered what had been implanted.

"They were leaders, masters of their own fate, as were all those in our species building efforts, but the human mind developed in a way we had never seen before. They were arrogant, demanding, selfish, absolutely positive that they alone were the masters of their world.

"It took only a short time for them to quarrel with each other, to hurt, maim, even kill each other, to force others of their kind into slavery, to steal and lie, to unfaithfully mate."

I was amazed at what Qadroth was saying, not because I was disagreeing, but because he seemed to be exactly right. He was talking about human beings from a deep knowledge, and I was embarrassed to listen to his allegations despite the fact I agreed with him. I also recognized this same arrogance in Riba, the same to a lesser degree in Qadroth himself. He was scowling at me again, and then continued his dissertation.

"It was my brother, Sonneth, who initially fertilized the human subspecies, and to this day, he regrets it. 'I took away their privileges,' he told me, 'and forced them to fend for themselves until their totally unkempt minds would allow them to return to our universal fold.'

"As all of us are vastly aware, since human Tom is with us today, and we can experience his scattered thought processes," there was general laughter at this point, "the Marquian mind has never evolved into the splendid examples we have created in other subspecies."

He wasn't smug or self-righteous at all, just simply stating a fact that was personally devastating. He did say something that intrigues me. He said that Sonneth, 'took away their privileges.' I wonder if Qadroth or Riba or, maybe any Quarian has that ability, that power to deny these other subspecies the ability to venture through time and space? What is it that makes the Quarian something special in this council or in this universe? Are they the leaders by birthright? Or, are we looking at master and slave? That thought is frightening in its entirety. If the Quarian created these subspecies, did the Quarian naturally assume superiority?

This would answer some of my questions about the way Riba talks with me, as if I had no part in a discussion. There is an arrogance in both Riba and Qadroth that I have found in humans that seem to think they are better than those around them. It's a selfish, egoistic problem found in many human cultures, and apparently at the universal level as well.

All eyes were on me. I've never been humiliated like this in my life. I can't run away because I don't know where I am, and this large, tall, eloquent being had just proclaimed that his brother was the God I have been worshiping for my entire life. There's something very wrong with this whole picture.

Most scientists are willing to accept that human ancestors probably evolved from members of the ape family, yes probably millions of years ago, but through some space traveler inseminating them on some wild sexcapade? Yes, I am insane.

"No, my friend, you are not insane, but after we find a successful answer to our current problem, I hope we will be able to convert you into the kind of being we were striving for so long ago."

My god, now the man is threatening me. Panic was starting to replace the fear of insanity, I have to get out of here, I have to leave now, and I don't know how.

"Please, human Tom. No one is threatening you, and it's very important that you stay with us. You are going to be a big help in solving our problem." Qadroth was actually smiling at me, being gentle with his words, and I could see softness in his eyes. At the same time, Riba reached over and gently squeezed my arm. Riba, that fierce old taskmaster was also being supportive. Calm me down, make me acquiesce, then destroy me. That must be their game. Qadroth had lots on his mind and he continued.

"As we are all aware now, besides this wonderful universe we populate and travel through and enjoy, there is a parallel universe that is evil in nature. Many of the beings that inhabit that universe wish to destroy us and what we have. When the great and omnipotent Clotero brought the forces of madness, often referred to as chaos, under control and developed universal laws of mathematics and physics, it was necessary, as we are so very aware, to create an opposite so the forces of one would play off the other and, therefore, be in harmony.

"As likes oppose and opposites attract, throughout our universe we have likes and opposites. Now, we find this is true even to the full universe. It seems what we call our universe is only half the picture. A parallel universe that is totally opposite of what we know is the other half, and if those that inhabit that opposite should succeed in their current endeavor to destroy our universe and us with it, in reality they will be destroying existence as we know it. They will be destroying the opposite of what keeps them from flying off into nothingness. A return to madness. A return to chaos."

He stopped for just a moment, took a deep breath while letting what he had said settle in with his audience. It certainly did catch my attention. Something was going to destroy the universe? But why would I be in any position to do anything about it? I'm a simple archeologist and writer. How on Earth could I protect or save the universe?

"Because of our populating efforts over the years, many of our subspecies have evolved in special ways, and I believe it's these differences that will force the beings from the nether-places back into their home realms. Let me give you an example of what I'm talking about. Human Tom, in your own words, please describe briefly what I've just outlined."

Oh, God. Where do I start? There's so much I've just learned, just heard about. Qadroth wants an answer now. Gods I've never heard of breeding with apes, people from another universe invading this one, travel through time and distance and space. I don't know what to do or what to say.

"Enough, human Tom. Enough." I looked around, everyone was holding his head and moaning, while Qadroth was chuckling to himself, and Riba, stern old Riba, was scowling at me. "You see that if a representative of the Marq system should meet some of these nether-people, as we're calling them, his totally cluttered thinking systems would destroy them on the spot."

Everyone broke out in laughter, and again I was humiliated before them all. What could I say?

Qadroth continued, "In ancient mythology, the nether places were of a distant world. The old people of your Marq galaxy still understood; Mythology is universally accepted fact, human Tom. Sometimes you think of the nether world as being an underworld, but in reality, it is an opposite universe, an example of hell, again, using your terminology."

He was a great teacher and philosopher, this Qadroth, and he had used a combination of humiliation and example to make his lesson clear. There was much I didn't understand, but despite his treatment of me, of humans in general, I was beginning to admire this Quarian from the galaxy, Tanso. Although both Qadroth and Riba were from the same galaxy, they were miles apart in personality. I feared Riba as much as I respected what he was able to do. I felt I would be able to actually be friends with Qadroth if things were just a bit different. If, for instance, I weren't mad as they come, if I could simply say, "hey, we're all human here", if I had any concept of what was going on.

I wonder where I am in relation to the Earth? I mean, when that deep cave turned into a meeting room, were we still on Earth, or did we travel through space and time to another galaxy? Where is Tanso? Where is this outer galaxy, Dosen II? They call the Milky Way, Marq, and there are millions of other galaxies in the universe, and these people seem to know many of them, actually seem to be from many of them. If I'm not a coo-coo bird, and I believe I am, then I'm about to begin one hell of a quest, a journey of universal proportions. It certainly wasn't fair to say it in that way, but maybe humor will let me relax some. Riba was glaring at me once again and I tried to calm my mind down. How on Earth can I be calm in this setting?

As many do, I have often daydreamed of traveling outside this world, visiting the moon, being weightless, having an extraordinary physical relationship in zero gravity. I have never seriously thought I would do it. Maybe what's happening is just my subconscious kicking in, maybe this is either just an elongated dream, or my subconscious has taken over and I'm mad as a coot. "Yes, Riba, I'm sorry, I'll try to subdue my mind."

Qadroth separated us into groups, keeping Riba and me together with the Sarcathian, Tene. "We must travel through the ages and through the galaxies, back and forth until we have located and dislodged all these nether-people, forcing them to return to their home universe.

"The one thing to watch for is something that has been observed but not substantiated. It appears they have an inability to traverse time with the quickness and agility we have. I would think the Marq system, and particularly the planet Earth would be a haven for them, since they cannot respond as we do. Humans are cynical and selfish to a fault and you can use this knowledge to wedge them out."

Qadroth was looking at me but at least not snickering during that last speech. He has a mean streak but can control it at will. Riba is blatantly dangerous, while Qadroth is clandestinely dangerous.

He hadn't even taken a breath after that embarrassing tirade and I found myself under that waterfall again, the one just outside the cavern, the time eight thousand years before my birth. Again, Riba stood inside the cave smiling indulgently at me. Again, I felt I would not have a chance to meet those responsible for the fanciful rock drawings. These intergalactic time travelers simply didn't recognize my need for understanding this part of human history.

"Come out from under the fountain, human Tom. We must begin what you are calling our quest." It was my time to smile. Riba may have a sense of humor after all. I stepped into the cavern and looked around at the rock walls, trying desperately to see some rock etchings. There weren't any at all, no etchings, no colorful drawings, no indication that indigenous people lived here. Disappointing is the best way to describe my current feelings.

This is a point of extreme universal energy. I understand that from all the stories and legends of the old people, so maybe it is avoided by the general population and reserved for shamans and the like. Maybe that's why there aren't any petroglyphs or any rock art inside the cave. Of course, just being in such a highly energized area should make me feel really good as a historian. Being with what I now believe are space and time travelers from other parts of our universe is unquestionably the most exciting thing that has ever happened to me.

We hear so often that without our history we could still be barbarians, that learning from history is what has allowed us to become civilized, and yet, are we? Politicians are accused of never learning from history, we often see major difficulties acted out in the same ways that brought turmoil, even anarchy and war eons before. Humans have a difficult time learning from history and at the same time we study history in every level of our education. To walk outside this little cavern and see one of the ancient dwellers of these parts actually chipping away at a rock would probably bring on a stroke or heart attack, but damn me I'd sure like to do that.

Another thought is dancing around my addled brain: how on Earth would I be able to write the story? An editor's guffaws would bring the walls in if I tried to write the story of discussing petroglyphs with one that made them. Then again, understanding their meaning would allow for an entirely different kind of article. Riba's eyes are burning holes in my head and I have to "let it go, Tom," without him actually saying it.

Maybe Qadroth and Riba are right, that we evolved into less than what had been expected. I don't like this kind of thinking, but I'm forced to look deep into my own soul to try and understand what is happening. Yes, I must accept that this Universal Council has a problem with what they are calling an invasion from a nether world, and at the same time I have to work on what I feel is most important to me, my world's history. How can I sit here in the sand, water dripping off me by the gallon and still be able to think about the human race after being told by some alien from some other galaxy that the human mind never evolved to some kind of universal perfection?

I'm looking at two problems and am fully capable of separating them into categories to be investigated. Why do they call this a problem? I can comprehend what Qadroth was saying about chaos, positives and negatives, and gods, but how the hell can I do anything about any of it? What's important to me right now is, I can do something about our knowledge of the ancient people of the earth if I'm really here. That's the real question, isn't it?

Chapter Four

Soaked to the skin again, I made my way into the cave and back to Riba and Tene in time to hear Tene say, "We do not know in which time these others may be, Riba. How will we be able to find them?"

My thoughts exactly, or almost exactly. We don't know very much about these nether-people, about who or what they are, why they feel it important to destroy this universe, or what their basic philosophies are. Before we can go on a search and destroy mission, we need to know a whole lot more about the quarry we're stalking. In order to find these people, we need to know who they are, inside. What makes them do things and think certain ways?

I caught Riba giving me a questioning look. "What is it, old one?"

"You have answered our first question, human Tom. Very good. I think to find the answers to those questions we must call on all our powers. Let's sit by the circle now and ask our keeper of time where the nether-people are. We can do this by knowing which period of time they entered our universe.

"Sometimes, human Tom, your senseless mind patterns do work in an orderly way. This was one of those times. Thank you." Old Riba wanted to smile, I could tell that, but he just wouldn't give me bragging rights beyond his 'thank you.' Who are these people I'm with? Are they cousins, or maybe Riba would be an uncle somehow, and Tene would be a cousin. I'll have to try and work that out. Relationship and language. I'm replacing my own quest for knowledge with their quest to stop the interlopers, and as always I'm trying to learn. Not once has anyone of these members of the Universal Council talked about their home life, their home planets, their likes and dislikes. It has just come to me that there isn't one single woman on the council. I hope that isn't by design.

When I was at the council table we were all dressed the same, everyone spoke perfectly clear English with no accents. This will continue to baffle me I'm afraid and take away from what I believe we are supposed to be doing. I'm accepting some of what seems to be happening and fighting like hell with other parts. Speaking a language that doesn't exist yet, all wearing the same kinds and styles of clothing without using a change room, knowing what each is thinking, conversing by thought alone are questions that can't just be answered with a yes or no.

An ability to move through space and time is something that physicists have discussed, at least the possibility of bending the concept of time, but to move through light years of space, that is, distance in the twinkling of an eye, even using the idea of wormhole travel is more than this puny little human mind can comprehend. There are more than five billion people on Earth and out of that number they picked me. Of course, I'm mad, loony, fruitcake, nuts.

Besides being mad as that hare we know about, or was it a hatter? Regardless, I would still like an answer. We're in a cave some eight thousand years before my birth. Three people, all related because a member of the Quarian tribe that Riba belongs to, ventured into the universe and mated with everything he could find. Tene from Sarcathia, I from Earth, God knows how many other subspecies, as they like to call us, are here because one guy had the hots for animals, or at the least sentient beings on other planets, in other times.

"Riba, when Sonneth traveled about the universe, creating subspecies, was there a philosophical goal? Was there a purpose, a pattern? Why would he attempt to mate with a species other than his own? I have these terrible pictures in my mind of this mad, sex crazed time traveler making it with strange animals, and I can't understand why?"

Riba had drawn his circle and made the separations and was getting ready to call in the gate keeper, but as I asked, he looked up at me with just a hint of a smile. "Your species, humans on the planet Earth, in the galaxy Marq, evolved into what you are today, human Tom, because of a deep philosophical belief held by us. When the universe was flying apart, chaos everywhere, madness with no meaning, our creator, you call him God, we know him as Clotero, brought meaning. His physics and mathematical laws allowed the universe to take its shape, allowed the galaxies to form and evolve, allowed suns to develop, and planets to cohere, and most importantly, allowed life forms to begin their long trek through time.

"You add levity where it isn't needed, my long suffering friend. When Sonneth began his journey through time and through the universe, his mission was spelled out in detail. Go forth and bring free thinking, free choice beings to the universe. Yes, human Tom, his travels took him to every galaxy with life forms, and in so many, he did pass our seed and bring forth a universe full of wonderfully evolved beings, diverse as the stars themselves, and all thinking, creating beings.

"I recognize what your chaotic mind is trying to tell you, but no, he did not go on a rampage of sexual splendor. Why you humans evolved the way you did, I can't answer. There is something in one of the genes that gives you this superiority complex, that makes you feel you must dominate at all times, that makes it so very difficult for you to understand how the universe is an inter relational concept. The concept of intelligence relating to evolvement has never come into discussion at our level, only in the human mind, and I think it's part of your selfish and greedy make up."

Riba is certainly not one to waste words, but in this case he is on the money when he discusses ego and selfish greed. Interesting to me, he didn't include the Quarians in that. They seem to have those same traits as I've witnessed so far. Humans have never treated each other with much respect more or less other creatures on the planet. He calls us selfish and greedy, I believe I have called us that in the most recent past, and there are so many ways to prove the point. The demise of passenger pigeons, the almost demise of the North American Bison, worldwide hunger except in certain countries, worldwide slavery, and I mean that, worldwide. Illegal immigrants trying to get ahead are put into slavery by way of holding their immigrant status over their head. We can go on and on proving Riba's statement, and it's not something I'm the least bit proud of.

Maybe this meeting with these people from other galaxies and planets and solar systems will lead to some answers to these questions. I can't imagine changing the human beings that exist, but maybe for future generations. Riba, almost but not quite glaring at me brings me back to this reality. He almost looks like he's going to say something like, "can we get on with this?' I just nod a smile at him and he turns his attention back to the circle in the sand.

He pressed the 'now' portion of the peace symbol look alike and we had a fourth sitting with us. A large and hairy fourth. Yeti. Bigfoot. Sitting at council with us. Standing, he was well over seven feet tall with a large head sitting on massive shoulders. Although his face was covered in hair, it was easy to discern its shape, with a strong jaw line and chin, but gently flattened nose, high strong brows, and large, sensitive eyes, brownish in color. Descriptions of Yeti I've read from Himalayan trekkers don't do justice to the real thing. This specimen is magnificent and I'm sitting next to him, unafraid, searching for some way to fully comprehend the situation.

47

All the legends I'd heard through the years are true. Yeti is the keeper of time, and all those tales of areas of high energy, of people passing into other dimensions, are true. For thousands of years, the original men on earth knew this and lived with earth as a friend. They knew differences between now and then and yet to come, communed with all things on Earth, and had religious philosophies tuned to this. What was it that changed humans from what Sonneth expected to what we are?

Yeti, Tene, and Riba were staring at me. Again.

"I'm sorry, but I can't help this thinking process. There are thousands of questions racing through my mind right now."

Sarcathian Tene wasn't angry or even upset as he replied. "Tom, on my planet, one whose mind splinters in a million pieces and can't be controlled is considered mad, but I understand what you are. You have just solved our problem of how to find the nether-people, and what their plan is for destroying our universe.

"We must now travel to the time when humans first started to change from living with knowledge and beauty to becoming selfish with intense egotism and, I'm sure Tom, this is where we will find the nether-people."

I'm beginning to understand that Sarcathians are much like Quarians, little sense of humor, all busy and full of business, and yet, not doing any of their own thinking. When I come with an idea or a thought, Tene understands and is able to discuss it, but the thought would never occur to him without outside help.

Riba and Qadroth do some abstract thinking but it appears that Tene does not. Is this true for all Sarcathians? I want very much to get to know some of these people, and I'm not doing a very good job of it. Or is it that they aren't letting me get to know them?

Yeti spoke slowly and with very little emphasis on any particular syllable. He sounded almost as we would expect a computer or machine to sound. "When the people, from what we now believe is the other side began to arrive, I was not going to let them through the gate, but they knew all the right things to say and do, even though they were not quite like us. They would go forward when they wanted to go back in time, and they were cruel, even to each other, much as the humans are now. I considered a long time, but finally had to let them through. As I look back on what was happening, I only considered these people to be slower than most and the idea that they were diametrically opposed to everything in this universe never entered my mind."

Yeti said, "like us." I wonder where the line is drawn. In ancient human history it has been accepted by some that there were individuals that could travel to what we always thought of as different dimensions. I wonder if the dimension, instead of being a different plane of existence, is instead, time. Shamans then could move through time, maybe even distance, and of course that would give them exceedingly strong powers within their tribe or group. Riba is scoring my brain with his scowls right now and Yeti is continuing to speak.

"This has been my mistake, Riba. I should have been more alert, but I was not aware of the problem. I first noticed changes in the way humans treated each other and it was about the same time I recognized changes in the way people were moving through time. Something should have been said, and I must stand responsible." Yeti's massive shoulders slumped downward, his brow was furrowed so deep I had trouble picking up his eyes, and if anything, he looked defeated.

"There is no reason for blame of any sort, Yannow." Riba was very kind, actually gentle as he continued. As I am around Riba more and more I find he is made up of many levels of feeling. When I thought of him, it was always on a single plane but that has changed considerably. There is feeling and humor, warmth, to a degree, and a desire to find the truth. He was talking to all of us now. "What we must do is find out as much as possible from you, Yannow and then venture to their time. What can you tell us?" Yeti has a name, Yannow, and it took just a moment for him to get his thoughts in order, something I had noticed over and over with Riba, Qadroth, and Tene. This is what they consider a controlled mind. Some things tucked away in some cobweb filled corner, and it takes an effort to release it. Not us uncontrolled humans, oh, no. We have a mind that clicks into place immediately, and Riba, don't you forget that.

"Just as you," Yannow started in his flat, even voice, "they look in the manner of those to where they travel. However, it is as if they do not want to look good, that is handsome in the manner of wherever they are. As if they wish to look somehow, ugly.

"In the same way we have fun with each other from time to time, teasing and joking, their jokes and teasing are designed to hurt. They take delight in being cruel."

For the life of me, as insane as I am at this moment, I can't picture a family of Yeti carousing and playing at a family picnic, playing hide and seek or kick the can or pin the tail on the...no.

Yannow continued, "It appears to me that they take great honor in lying, as we take honor in telling the truth."

Saying that brought a flash, a great truth. "Riba, I would guess these nether-people came to this planet within the first million years of human evolvement, not as an invasion, but in small groups, and bred with various tribes and societies, injected their nether genes, and altered human evolvement.

"It seems to me that they feel changing the evolution of the human would change the entire universe and thus destroy it. I don't know if my thinking is straight here, Riba, but if you did not allow humans into the universal family because of their altered evolution, then the nethers would not be accomplishing their goals. Riba, my old friend, we're on the wrong planet. We won't find what we're after on Earth."

All three were fully engrossed in what I was saying. "Tom is right, Riba. The nethers are in another part of the universe trying to implant some other system right now. And we wouldn't let humans in the Universal Council? Riba, we need to call another council meeting. Our focus is wrong here." The all-business Tene, scowling as Riba might, but for a different reason, again understood the answer without conjuring the question himself.

How far I've come in...well, I can't answer that can I? Time means nothing now, but I have learned so much about what it means to be human, not just human, but a universal entity, and I've made some fine friends. The God I've been loving all these years is the right God, I just didn't have the whole story. Sonneth brought Quarian genes to those of the great apes at the behest of Clotero, God of the universe, but in fact, Clotero had created an opposite universe, the people of that place are behind the strange differences between humans and those who populate other galaxies. Time for my new Universal Council friends and apparently those from an opposite universe is just as relative as Einstein attempted to teach us. What's a million years between friends, eh?

I'm sitting in the sand surrounded by people from other galaxies and a being that many are willing to say doesn't exist, and what we're discussing is making sense. Madness is a strange malady, I guess, because I'm willing at this moment to travel with these people wherever it might take us, to do whatever is necessary to bring our universe back into its proper alignment with its opposite. The one question that must prove I'm nuts is simply this: why me?

Is the nether world hell?   Bad is good, ugly is beautiful?   To create havoc and chaos is the highest attainment?   I wonder why I had to go mad in order to understand life. In the human it seems that ego could be the driving force and, coupled with selfishness, has allowed him to rule his planet.   Subservient animals, even other humans as slaves are needed to feed that ego. Am I a typical human, one that could be a stand-in for five billion others?

That is an answer I fear because even now as we sit in the sand in this cold, damp cave, I'm thinking of the ancient people and their attempts at preserving history through scratching on rocks.   I want to be outside there, looking for them and that has to be a form of selfishness feeding my ego that wants to be the first to decipher petroglyphs.   I'm sitting close enough to touch Yeti, close enough to hold a discussion with him, and my thoughts are wandering to my desire to understand an ancient culture when I am beginning to understand a universal culture.

Of course, it all makes sense when you're mad.

Chapter Five

Another movement through time and space, never a clue to prepare for the journey, just one moment sitting with Yeti and company, and the next, back before the Universal Council.   Soul jarring is the effect, more than what happens following a major international flight through time zones and having to come back to reality through a process called jet lag.   Am I the first human with galaxy lag? Why didn't we just walk through the cave as we did the first time I met the council?   I have entered so much data my head will hurt for months if I mentally survive what is happening.

Interesting, I can't help but wonder at what period of time, relative to my birth, we're in at these Council sessions?   In the cave, ten seconds ago, it was eight thousand years before my birth.   All I know right now, this is my reality, Riba is speaking, and many eyes seem to be taking me apart, cell by cell.   Riba just explained to the Council what took place in the cavern, that place of wonder along the banks of ancient Lake Lahontan.   I think he takes pleasure in pointing out it was "the totally skewed mind" of a human that unraveled the mystery of the nether-people.

"We think we know why they did what they did not too long after humans came into existence.   It's what they are attempting even today that is most frightening."   These meetings are quiet affairs, with members often commenting by way of their minds, rather than vocally, and the problem with that is, I can't take part in the dialogue.   They understand what I'm thinking, but I can't understand them. Riba has done a fine job explaining what we discussed in the cave with Yannow, but I'm left without knowing what any of the members of the council might have to say about the matter.   From the looks on many of their faces, there is a discussion going on, and it doesn't include any of my thoughts.

All this brings me to an idea that has been bumping around my head. It seems it is only the Quarians that run things in this universe. It is Quarians that inseminated all those other species to create us subspecies, it is Quarians that run these council meetings, it is Quarians that seem to lead all the discussions, and let's not forget it is Quarians that determined humans ineligible for membership here. Strange that none of the other subspecies speak up with ideas and thoughts. It isn't just the Sarcathians that aren't free thinkers, as humans are, it is all the other subspecies. Why do the Quarians have so much control?

We are told that when one controls another the outcome is usually disastrous. Think about relationships between men and women, control often leads to abuse, which often leads to physical harm. Do the Quarians control these council meetings and everything else in the universe to such an extent that the other subspecies are reduced to saying, "yes, sir, master, sir"? Are the other subspecies slaves to an extent?

"Well, it's obvious to me," Qadroth picks up the commentary as Riba finishes his comments. "The human population has been inseminated with nether genes, and I agree with Riba and human Tom, that they are attempting to spread their seed to other galaxies. The burning question remains, what do we do about it?" There was a brief moment of contemplation by Qadroth and the other members before he continued.

"We can't go back to the time when they implanted the humans and simply change that. No, there have been too many years and too much history. Too many generations would be destroyed, history altered, to do that.

"Human Tom, you have performed a magnificent service to the universe, even with your unkempt mind, and I would like you to stay on with us and help solve this problem. You seem to work well with Riba and Tene, and I would welcome you to the Council."

My unkempt mind, as Qadroth put it, is excited by this prospect for two reasons. First, they actually asked, didn't simply make a statement as before, but more importantly, I'll feel far better working with Riba and the Council knowing I really am wanted, that they desire my input not cringe from my inner musing. This is a turning point for me, and I think, with only a few exceptions, I won't even contemplate whether or not I'm completely insane. I just nod my head in the direction of Qadroth and get a gentle smile from him.

He is a leader from every aspect of the term. Qadroth is regal in appearance, but with a gentle quality that Riba could learn from, and an ability to grasp meaning as they are discussed in council. On Earth, I think Qadroth would be someone that many would want to have making decisions. I'm very proud to know I'm going to be working with him at his request.

Everyone here knows everyone else, and I'm the lone wolf, so to speak, not knowing most at the table, and having no idea where in the sky to look for the various galaxies these folks represent. I remember looking for some of the prominent constellations through my little "space adventurer" telescope when I was a youngster, but right now I don't even know where I am. I wonder what the Big Dipper looks like from where I am right now.

Hell, maybe one of the stars in the Big Dipper is the galaxy that I'm in right now. Riba is glowering at me and I know once again I've interrupted the program. "Sorry. I'll try to remember not to think too much." I know that won't happen. I can't get the question of the Big Dipper out of my mind. It's like hearing a stupid jingle and your mind repeats it a thousand times.

The Council seemed pleased at my decision to join them and even old Riba gave me a pleased look as if to say he applauded my acceptance. One of those at table was a fat little guy, jolly as the day, and quite friendly, named Rohn-Da. He had been very attentive during Riba's and Qadroth's presentations and was among the first to come to me. From the Torry system, Rohn-Da also had a serious side.

"Tom, when this is all over, I'd like it if you could come to my home and meet some of the people there. We aren't like the Quarian, all business and important, and we're not like the Sarcathians either, with their veritable logic. I think probably, we are more like you humans, or at least what you humans might have been if your history hadn't been altered. Will you give that some thought, my friend?" I think Rohn-Da could actually see a little fear in my demeanor as I answered him. I know as he spoke I was filled with fear.

"Rohn-Da, is it possible that the nether-people would want another species like humans in order to continue their attempt to destroy the universe? What I'm getting at, my new friend, is this: Would they attempt to implant the people of Torry before one of the other systems? It seems to me they went to Earth for a reason. What is there about humans that drew them, and is that same thing true for those from Torry?" It was my turn for some contemplation while Rohn-Da digested my last comments.

The only thing I know about Torry is that Rohn-Da is very much like humans on earth and I wonder if all those from that system are similar. God knows humans are as different from each other as possible, but there are traits we all share. If those from the other side were looking for something that is similar in Torrians and humans, they could very well be invading Rohn-Da's home system right now. How many other of these subspecies are there that share similar traits to humans and Torrians? How many other galaxies are in jeopardy from this invasion?

Am I too involved in all this? Is it real? My God, I'm only a simple guy who likes to live in the desert, write stories about the old people, and take pictures of where they lived. Why am I the one they picked, the one Riba chose, to be the human representative in this universal tragedy? I know deep in my soul this must be reality, it can't just be insanity, there's too much for one mad mind to simply conjure. Maybe it wasn't the taking of one's life that Shakespeare contemplated with his "to be, or not to be," but rather the question was what part of reality to accept.

I'm wringing wet, not from that waterfall at the cave but from perspiration. My mind is actually tired as I try to put some kind of meaning to what is going on around me. Time and space travelers from two universes are in a monumental struggle for survival and they call on me to help? I'm actually the one that has come up with a few of what appear to be answers? No one has done any creative, critical thinking about this problem, and yet they are supposed to be the leaders of the known universe. This is very difficult to understand, and when I get alone with either Riba or Rohn-Da I'm going to have to press them for some answers.

I can see now what those thoughts of mine were trying to say during the council deliberations just moments ago. I could see what humanity might have looked like had it not been altered. Rohn-Da is the essence of a human minus the influence of the nether gene. If my thoughts are correct, I hope they are more wrong than I've ever been, but if they are correct, the nether people are on Torry right now implanting their corrupt ways. Would we be as jolly folk as Rohn-Da if not for the interference so many centuries ago? Would we have a rightful place at the council table? Centuries of slavery and slave trading, centuries of hateful bigotry and religious intolerance, centuries of fear of neighbors, and centuries of war and killing have altered the human existence, and it's all because of the nether gene implanted so long ago.

Rohn-Da brought me back to this reality from my brief reverie. "Riba, can you and Tom come to Torry with me? I mean, right now. I think Tom's right about the nether-people coming to my home system. Will you?"

Damn, they did it again. Standing in the Council chambers, all those stone walls and hard floor, the warm little fire pit, and that wonderful divan, contemplating life's tragedies one second, standing on a rural path in some Torrian village the next. If nothing else comes from all this, I must learn how they do it. I wonder if such a thing as getting credit for miles exists. Riba did not think that was funny. I don't think these things in order to get to the old Aztec, but if I could, I would. He glares and fumes, and there really isn't a thing I can do about it, except, of course, to enjoy the consequences of my thoughts.

Torry is just as Rohn-Da described, with greens and blues radiating through the cloud-filled sky, reds and yellows, in every hue and shade, emanating from plants, shrubs, and trees, splashed across the landscape.

We're standing on a magnificent plain, rolling hills covered in trees and brush, a broad sky filled with the fleece of running lambs, an area endowed with beauty, and apparently, peace. I've seen pictures of Earth taken from satellites and from the moon, and I've always considered my planet, my home, absolutely gorgeous. It was the first pictures taken in the vicinity of the moon that created the term "The Big Blue Marble," and I can imagine what this planet would look like from a couple of hundred thousand miles away.

There are no other people around, no signs of civilization other than this pathway, and that seems rather strange since Rohn-Da said we were going to his home and his family. Maybe these people don't live in buildings as I would know them. I can almost see the rolling pleasure of a western Pennsylvania landscape, giant oaks and hardwoods, grasses knee deep in meadows filled with cattle and horses, cabins holding families that fill history books with names we all know. This could very well be some spot on earth but my mind is much more interested in this planet in the Torry Galaxy.

As we look at various planets and moons in our solar system, it always appears to me that they are peaceful, almost benign. It's on landing one discerns the problems. The moon, Mars, Venus, are not habitable for humans. How did the Earth come about the way it has? I wonder if I will find some answers in these travels I'm making. I'm already learning huge amounts about the various people in the universe, things that no one on Earth has a clue about.

The concept of life other than that on earth has filled libraries, driven television programs, made scientists drool with expectation, and here I am, standing on another planet in another galaxy with representatives from two galaxies, and Riba wants me to control my thinking. Impossible, old friend, impossible.

Some of the questions that have been nudging my brain cells around during my time with Riba and the council members are coming back to me now. We aren't talking about planetary systems at the universal council table. We're talking about entire galaxies. I can't understand the size of the Milky Way, can't understand how many suns and planets there might be, how can I begin to understand a universe? Two universes? How many suns with planets within the Milky Way are also teeming with humanoid life? I have to find the time to get these answers or I will end up in the mental ward of some hospital on some planet in some galaxy somewhere.

"Rohn-Da, there is nothing on Earth to compare with this beauty. The intensity of the colors almost overwhelms and the variety of plants is amazing. A botanist must have to be schooled forever just to absorb the number. Rohn-Da, you have a beautiful home. Thank you for inviting me here."

"Your words are appreciated, Tom. We've arrived in my own time and we're just a few minutes from where I live. I think we should go there and plan our next move. Besides, my wife is expecting me for dinner and she'll be delighted to see Riba again.

"Riba, you're strangely quiet.   What is it, time traveler?"

Rohn-Da just did something I've not seen in any of the other subspecies. He picked up on what we might call a vibe.   Something Riba was contemplating but hadn't put into thought for Rohn-Da to fully understand. Humans can see this through such things as body language, and apparently so can those from Torry.

"Human Tom is seeing your planet for the first time and is able to describe the beauty that I see but have never expressed. Is it that I can't express beauty? Or is it that we Quarian are also a bit arrogant and contemptuous, as we accuse the humans? Food for thought, eh Rohn-Da?" This is the closest I've been to the thinking process that drives the old Aztec. Riba is deeply philosophical it seems when he drops his guard. There is a real person there, and it took a visit to such a warm and friendly planet such as Torry to bring it out. I'm glad I was here to see it first-hand. He continued, expressively, but not quite so philosophically.

"The last time I visited you and Tanda, she fed me until I thought I would burst, and then your daughters danced for us. As I recall, a bit too much Torry wine found me on the dance floor as well." My old friend Riba, stern faced and demanding, tipsy on wine and dancing? I hope to see that again.

"Human Tom, you are the first of your subspecies to visit this fine planet, even this galaxy, so don't be surprised if you are covered with questions.   Of course, with the human mind never slowing down, going at full speed in hundreds of directions at the same time, our hosts may not be able to get a question in, eh Rohn-Da?"

The two chortled at their little joke but Riba's comments awoke more questions in me. "Rohn-Da, I see tremendous beauty, there is no doubt, but where are we right now in relation, say to an industrial center or large city? This appears to be very rural in nature. How big are your cities?" My questions could go on for another hour, but I must give the little guy time to answer.

"There are areas in which we congregate for the opportunity to mix with one another, but I don't know what you mean by the words cities and industrial center. What are they?" This certainly took me by surprise.

"An industrial center is where commerce takes place, where goods are manufactured and distributed. Cities are where people live and work, and often have industrial centers within them. Where do most of your people live?" Rohn-Da just stood there with the strangest look on his face.

"I simply don't understand, Tom. We live everywhere. I don't know what you mean by commerce or manufactured. I'm sorry, Tom, we'll have to discuss this later, because I just don't know what you're talking about."

A society, a planet with no commerce, and with no population centers for industry? What about politics and government? I'm amazed and it doesn't look like I'm going to get any answers from Rohn-Da, he seems as bewildered as I, right now. Riba tried to help, but of course, he has such a low regard for humans and life on Earth it probably didn't help the Torrian at all.

"On Earth, Rohn-Da the people live in houses as you do, but they are nestled one up against another, with streets and highways going every which way. Well, you wouldn't know what a street or highway is anyway would you? I guess you and Tom will have to work this out your own way.   I can't explain most of what I've found on Earth."

We turned in at a gravel lane and walked toward a large edifice, not a house, as we would call it on Earth, but a building for sure.   Built as a series of cylinders, some larger than others, and butting so as to connect, the building sported at least three levels, maybe four, and there were many windows on each story, seeming to look out toward every direction.   The same vivid colors as the plants and trees were used as base and decoration with seemingly geometric patterns created combining the architecture and ornamentation.   It was very surrealist, and very exciting.   If these warm and gentle Torrians have architecture as delightful as this, their other forms of artistic adventure must be truly delightful. Oh, my.   I'm finding myself more enthralled with the culture every minute.

Stone fences surround the building and well cared for yards.   The gardens were planted in the same patterns and decorations as the home, and the whole was a brilliant mass of color and design.   The gardens were filled with large and small plants, some with magnificent flowers, others not.   I couldn't help but wonder whether or not I was looking at an edible garden or just a decorative one.

"Rohn-Da, I'm overwhelmed by the beauty and color.   If Riba, that old scoundrel who drinks wine and dances his nights away, ever lets me get home, I'm going to try and duplicate these colors and patterns.   I must bring you to Earth to see some of the beauty we have.   Our trees are of so many different types and sizes, but nothing compared to what you have here.   I'm not sure I would ever be able to describe your flowers and shrubs."   There were rolling hills in all directions and what appeared to be great thriving forests massed on many of the hills.   Off in the distance, I can't judge distance right now, but several miles away there were high mountains, some with frostings of snow and ice at their peaks, and again the deep greens and blues that generally mean large flourishing forests. "Overwhelming beauty," was all I could say.

Many of the shrubs were climbers and they scrambled all over the various cylinders that make up the home, their tentacles grabbing at whatever was available, flinging themselves on dancing currents, falling a bit, only to catch on something else, making it a platform for another swan attempt. The flowers, while more restricted rambled about offering vibrant color and wonderful perfume to the air. "Rohn-Da, will you come and visit my planet as I'm visiting yours?"

The chubby little Torrian had me by the hand and was saying there was nothing in the world he'd rather do. "That will be an experience, Tom. Oh my, yes, I'll come to your home planet. Look, my family." Three lovely ladies had emerged from the building and were walking toward us, smiling as broadly and openly as Rohn-Da himself.

"Tom, please say hello to my wife Tanda, and my lovely daughters Tetta and Cor-ah. Ladies, let me introduce Tom. He's from Earth. Yes, Earth, he's a human from the Marq system." He stood so proud with his family as he said this, and they responded as Riba said they might, with oohs and ahhs, and gasps of delight, and accompanied with genuine smiles of welcome.

Interesting, but this is the first time age has entered my mind. I have no more idea than anything how old Riba might be, or Rohn-Da, and now I'm meeting Rohn-Da's wife and daughters. On Earth, I would estimate Riba to be 450-years-old, just kidding, old one, and Rohn-Da to be maybe 40. The daughters would be about early 20's on Earth. Well, for sure, full grown women of magnificent stature and form.

One at a time, each of the women grabbed little Riba and hugged him until I thought they might break the old Aztec, and then they turned their attention to me, walking around, smiling, looking closely, seeing all the resemblances that I saw in Rohn-Da, and saying, "hello, how are you?", "nice to have you here", "a real human, wow". My eyes were full of them, as well. Rohn-Da's wife Tanda was at least as tall as I, making her a tower next to her chubby little husband. Her long, deep red hair and flashing gray green eyes, strong jaw line, and wide friendly smile were enough to make my knees weak, and add a Hollywood star's body to the mix, and I was very glad to be on Torry.

Everything I've seen since becoming a universal traveler indicates that most of the species seem to be anatomically related. With Tanda, it was obvious. We all have two arms and two legs, two ears and two eyes, and, oh yes, the women do seem to have two lovely breasts. Tanda's daughters looked much like their mother, hair, stature, and all the other parts just described, and the entire family had the warm smile of papa Rohn-Da. Riba, as usual, brought me back to this reality.

"You must learn to accept the totally uncontrolled mind of the human. They have not evolved as the rest of us and simply let their thoughts go swinging wildly through the ether, not caring an iota who might intercept them.

"Tom, to answer one of your questions, yes, the Torrian women are the dominant sex, being larger and stronger than their males, and doing most of the work. Men are able to do some of the more menial tasks, and the work that doesn't take a large amount of strength, but mostly, it's the women who run things here."

"And the men like it that way," Rohn-Da interjected immediately, accompanied by laughter from him and his family. "I could never take care of a place like this by myself. I need these wonderful women." Tanda reached out and pinched her husband, ever so tenderly, right on his fat little butt. There was love between them. "My wife understands, and more, she supports my position on the Council."

That brought me back to that question I had in the cave recently. "I've noticed there aren't any women on the Universal Council. Is there a reason for that? On Earth, we insist on equal opportunity for men and women and there would be serious consequences if women were denied a seat on the council simply because of their sex."

It was Riba who answered the question and forthrightly, I might add. "There are many women leaders in the universe, Tom, and each of the planets and the various subspecies are responsible for who sits on the council. At the present time, two of the members are women, but from galaxies in which there isn't much physical difference to discern. You didn't recognize them, that's all."

Tanda got right into the conversation as well. "I sit on the Torrian Assembly as First Representative, and it was determined following a planet wide vote that Rohn-Da would be one of our representatives on the Universal Council. I'm afraid that most Torrian women are a little too aggressive for such a position." There was general laughter among the group, and although I didn't understand the joke, I was glad to hear the answers I got.

As we walked toward their home, Cor-ah took me by the hand, a gesture I enjoyed immensely, and when I squeezed gently, acknowledging the offer, she squeezed back. My heart was racing as we entered the home, and thoughts of Cor-ah were replaced by what was before me. Colors much softer than those I found outside, but just as vibrant. I think what I was seeing was a depth of color not just a hue or finish. These colors were almost three dimensional in appearance and I felt I could reach right into a wall or sill. Each room had a dominant color theme, walls and furniture, even decorative items expertly coordinated in shades. My feet were absorbed in rich carpeting and the air had an aroma reflective of the garden. Enchanting is the first word that came to mind and I went around what must have been the living room brushing my hand over lush furnishings, tapestry, plants, even bent down and felt the full throat of the loom. All my new galactic friends stood by while I did this. I wonder how they would react if we moved from this dimension to my own and I introduced them to my apartment in Virginia City.

This can't possibly be. My new galactic friends? Move from this dimension to another? A very bright light will shine in my eyes in a moment and I'll be beaten into submission.

The lights. Just as in the council chambers, free floating, seeming to be in the right place, to shed their light on a painting, on a vase, or on where we were. They moved with us, not the least intrusive, but not seeming to be connected to anything. Yes, the same lights I found, first in the cavern, then the council chambers. How long ago was that? When, compared to my birth, is now? Then I caught Riba glaring at me and realized the whole bunch was standing still, just staring at me.

"What's wrong? What have I done?"

"Human Tom, we must try to teach you how to dissect your thinking processes. We can't talk when your mind is so active." First, the glare from the old man and now he was laughing out loud. At me? Maybe just the easing of tension, but I think this is the first time I've heard Riba laugh. It struck my funny bone at the same time and, I guess, the whole Rohn-Da clan as well. It took a couple of minutes for all the giggling and snickering to settle down, but there was a definite relieving of tension.

They had never met a human, and now one was in their home, and they were being subjected to all my thoughts. "I'm sorry, it's just me. I'm trying to put all this in my memory, in some kind of context. So many new things, so many new places, so many new people, my own mind is overwhelmed. I'll try to maintain. I really will."

Tanda had mixed some drinks and was passing them around. "Wow. What is this?"

Riba had his glass, gave me a knowing smile, and asked me the same question. "What would you call it, Tom?"

"You know, it has the quality of what I would call beer, maybe a little like an ale, but not quite as potent as a stout. Am I close?" It was good and I knew it had to be one of the drinks of choice on Torry.

"It was originated here, Tom, but has traveled throughout the universe. Do you think it might have been introduced on Earth before the problems?" Rohn-Da seemed reluctant to come out and say before humans were thrown out of the Universal Council, but Riba went on and answered anyway.

"I'm sure it was. On Earth now, they enjoy what they call beer, and it's found in just about every culture, handed down from the time Clotero allowed the human to come into existence." He's right, of course, I was remembering some ancient history. Beer and wine were among the first things humans got right. Mead, fermented honey, if I remember right, and the changes that grains go through became beer and ale. Of course, some of the stronger things came a little later.

"Well, when I get a chance to bring you to Earth, my new friend, I'll see to it you get your fair share of our beer." Riba again became the stern old Aztec, the time traveler I know best.

"I think you ladies may have to excuse us now for a short time. We're here on a mission of great importance, and it's time for some planning."

I'm fully absorbed now, without a doubt, and I'm anxious for us to get started, to find out if these nether-people, as we insist on calling them, exist, and if so, are they here on Torry? I'm also amazed that there are so few differences between all of us, until I remember what Yeti said.   Something about becoming as those who live where you wish to be.   I've become used to the changing in dress based on where I am and whom I am with.   Right now, I'm dressed as a Torrian, but in council I was dressed as all the other council members, and at the cave, I was dressed as I, as Tom.

Is Rohn-Da then, this chubby little guy I like so much, or is he, in his own reality, a giant with three heads, two of which breathe fire?   Are Tetta and Cor-ah delightful and beautiful Torrian girls, or the daughters of a multi-bodied dragon?   The question though can be turned another way.   What do I look like in their eyes?   Since I am the one who entered their reality, I must, therefore, look as they do.   Maybe I'm the dragon.

Cor-ah again reached out and took my hand, gave it a gentle squeeze and whispered, "Thank you for thinking I'm attractive in your eyes.   I feel the same about you, Tom, but there is one thing.   You must remember that your every thought is in our heads as well.   Just so you know, daddy isn't a dragon and I don't have two heads."   She had a tinkley little laugh that was refreshing. It sprinkled good humor that bounced off all the walls of the living room. Then she narrowed her brow and continued, "If you keep up, mama will make you stand outside until you calm down."   It was a very humorous and gentle way of rebuking my behavior, and I squeezed her hand back.

"It wouldn't be nice to be banned to the garden if I couldn't   also   enjoy   your   graciousness   and   beauty. Interesting that you say I might be sent to stand outside. Our buildings on Earth are mostly square or rectangular, and when youngsters misbehave, they are often told to stand in the corner."   There was a large, open, gracious smile from Cor-ah, but it was time to go to work.   Tanda reached out and took Riba by the hand.

"Sweet Riba.   When do you ever come to visit that it isn't business?   You must come sometime and just relax.

Walk in the woods, watch the stars, listen to the sounds of water moving through the creek.

"Well, work it is for you, then.   I'll call when dinner's ready, and don't go off somewhere without telling me. Rohn-Da, I mean that."

By her tone, there was no doubt in my mind she meant what she said.   Little papa bear gave his wife a big smile and hug and led us off into another one of the cylinders.   I got an invitational smile and wink from Cor-ah as we left the room.   Was I reading something into that smile?   Or was she just being friendly to a guest?   If none of this is real, if this is madness as I've contemplated, then this is the right way to lose one's mind, on a planet filled with beautiful and lovely people, being flirted with by a charming young woman.

"I think human Tom is right to think the nether-people are here, or are planning to come here.   Since young Torrians have not been exhibiting any of the evolutionary problems we see in humans, it might mean they have not arrived or are in the process of arriving.   Rohn-Da, are there any outlying areas on the planet where these people could come, yet where enough interaction between the nether-people and your people would ensure the proliferation of their problematic genes? Where they would be free to spread the nether-people's genetic code around the globe?"   I was trying to remember that he didn't understand the concept of a city, so where would there be an area with a large local population?

"There are a group of islands in the sea to the north of here called Toland, near the equator, where the local population isn't too large, yet where their children tend to come to the mainland to better their economic and personal situations.   They then marry and rarely return to the islands except to visit.

"Toland is also a tourist area, so there are many visitors who, I believe, could also then return to their homes after possibly having relations with a nether person. These tourists also come from other galaxies in the universe, so it might just be a prime location to find these nether universe visitors."

"It would take two or three generations, Rohn-Da, but I don't see any great hurry from the nether-people. If we visited Toland, would human Tom stand out too much? Would his uncontrolled mind just be too obvious?"

"No. Those who live on Toland find the atmosphere and living conditions considerably slower than on the mainland, like tropical climates everywhere affect people everywhere. If something is said, we can simply say he's been working too hard and his mind isn't quite what it should be. We wouldn't be lying." Rohn-Da looked over at me as if to excuse the comment, a slight smile playing at the sides of his mouth, but continued. A quick glance at Riba found that smug little smile dancing in his face as well. You'll get yours, old man, you will.

"We can take one of the quick shuttle jumps there tomorrow if you think we're right in our thinking."

"All right then, we'll leave tomorrow. Human Tom, it's important for you to just be yourself. I guess I'll have to simply call you, Tom, as I've noticed Rohn-Da and his family already do.

"From the smells coming from below, I think we wrapped this up just in time. Tanda has fixed roast dorly, hasn't she? I love roast dorly." Riba was almost dancing at the prospect and, for the first time, he actually gave me a big pat on the shoulder as if we were buddies going out for a cold one.

"That's what she stuffed me with on our last visit, Rohn-Da, roast dorly. I think I ate two whole ones. Tom, this will be a treat for you." Riba was walking on his toes with excitement. I've never seen this side of him, and it must be an influence from this Torrian family, letting his natural Quarian guard slip aside. He took the stairs two at a time as we moved down one level and back into the dining area where a feast was laid out for us.

On a large table, with seats for all, was set plate after plate of food, none of which I'd ever seen before, but the aroma certainly woke my taste buds. When had I eaten last? I couldn't remember, and how long has it been since Riba and I left my little apartment in Virginia City? Time seems to have no meaning to me now, while before I was seriously ruled by the clock. There was always a deadline. Start the day with breakfast at six, work till noon, and the editors screaming about being late with copy and photos. Now, I couldn't begin to tell you what time it is, based on whatever sun is shining, or what day compared to Earth time, and I know for a fact I have no idea where I am, so it doesn't matter anyway.

If one played his cards right, he could use this time travel in a wonderful way, such as breakfast, travel here and a little back in time for breakfast, and then again, and again. I would weigh three hundred pounds in no time at all. I wonder what those ancient people that pecked their history into rocks ate for breakfast. Did they eat three times a day or only when food was available? Riba is giving me hell with those penetrating eyes of his. Okay old man, okay.

This item called a dorly, which seemed to enthrall Riba appears similar to a chicken, a chicken that is with four legs and no wings. It has large thighs and legs, breasts as a bird might, and then, large shoulders as well. Interesting to look at, but I must agree with Riba, it smells delicious. It appeared the table held enough food for many more than the six of us.

"Tom, will you sit next to me? I'll try to explain what some of our food is. It must be quite different from what you have on Earth." Cor-ah graced me with a wonderful smile and we settled in next to each other while the rest of the group took their places. At least the utensils were similar, but the plates seemed to be naturally warmed, and were translucent. Not glass and not plastic as I would know it.

"These dorlies, roasted like this, are so tasty, Tom. I roasted them with some fine pigglies and plenty of just, and then of course made the sauce with the drippings and more just." Tanda was a good cook and knew it, but I probably looked like some forlorn little boy from some dirty alley somewhere. I knew not what she was saying.

A frown came across Cor-ah's face. "Riba, darling, friend, this isn't going to work. Tom doesn't have the slightest idea what mama's talking about."

"It's okay Cor-ah, from the moment I met Riba, I haven't had the slightest idea of what was going on." That lightened the mood even more at the table, and everyone started talking at once, explaining what was what on the table. Finally I had to stop them.

"I'll make a deal with all of you. Nothing here will relate to anything on Earth, so if I discover I really like a pigglie, I'll ask Cor-ah to explain it to me. It all smells so very good, I know I'll like it all." The general uproar at the table calmed down and I was amazed at what happened next.

Cor-ah asked if I would like a little bit of each item, and as soon as I agreed, small helpings of each type of food on the table appeared on my plate without anyone moving. How could that be? Can their minds be so strong as to move items about with almost no effort? Extraordinary. I could picture a night club act featuring a sleight of hand performance like this. It would be worth millions on Earth, with TV contracts and live performances every night. How on Earth did that happen?

"It will take me a little time to get used to you, Tom." Cor-ah was looking straight into my eyes again, and that giddy feeling traveled up and down my body, a feeling I can't even try to explain other than to say, this girl is hitting on me, and I love it. "Your mind is so much fun, but it will take a bit of time to get used to it. Tom, I'd never try to hit you."

"Oh, God. I forget you pick up every thought. "Hitting on me" is a human phrase that shouldn't be taken literally. It means you're interested in me, possibly romantically." Now I've done it. She'll think I'm really a dork. Or a dorly.

Well, actually, I am a dork. It was my turn to just stare into her eyes and we smiled and just sat still for a moment. "You've not seen our ways before, Tom, so now I want you to watch your wine glass." It was hard, but I turned back to the table and watched as my wineglass slowly filled, and an equal amount disappeared from the decanter. I know my eyebrows went way up on my forehead, and I know my eyes opened pretty damn wide.

Rohn-Da brought us all back to some sort of reality. "It must be really different living on Earth if something as simple as serving dinner or pouring wine was so astonishing." Riba was choking back his humor as best he could and tried to explain what earth was like for him.

"Life on Earth," he said, "is so unlike that on any of the other planets in the Universal Council, it would amaze you. The mind talk you're hearing from Tom is a normal function. Everything on the planet is done physically, not by the strength of the mind. Even all travel, which by the way is done in the single plane of now, is done physically, with vehicles that physically have to be operated. The humans on Earth evolved separately from the other subspecies of the universe, and it wasn't until we started investigating this threat from the nether world that we discovered why." He looked to our host Rohn-Da to continue to explain what he was talking about. It was obvious the ladies were interested in the situation at hand.

"You see, when Clotero brought order from the madness, he brought into existence two complete universes, one the opposite of the other. Our bad is their good and so on. But, and here is where this delicious mind of Tom's comes into play. Tom recognized this total opposition, one from the other, and also discovered many of the same discrepancies in the human situation that could be attributed to a mingling of the subspecies human and a species from the nether universe. Tom believes the other side is trying to infiltrate this universe and destroy it by mating with other subspecies in the Universal Council."

One thing I've learned during my short time on this planet, Torrians have quick minds and can pick up on a subject or idea immediately. It was Tanda who asked if that was why the three of us are here. "You think those other people are here on Torry, don't you?"

"That is true, my wife, that is the sad reason we're here. Tom seems to think because there are so many similarities between the people of Earth and the people of Torry, that the nether-people may come here to infest our people. In fact, may already be here." His eyes were sad, dripping to the sides, his mouth was sad, his chubby little jowls actually drooped as he spoke. "In the morning, we will be starting our search." It was Cor-ah who surprised me the most.

"Without sounding like I'm rattling my own cage here, but I think you all agree that I have the strongest mind among us. Don't take this personally, dear Riba, but I am even stronger than you. I want to go with you. Three men, two representing the Universal Council and one from a planet no one has ever visited, well, you'll be a mystery, and you'll generate a lot of questions no matter where you go." She had a firm set to her jaw as she spoke, and it was obvious to me why the women of Torry were the dominant sex. They simply were stronger. Maybe that's what Tanda was saying about the women being too aggressive to sit on the Universal Council.

"If I'm along, then we're simply sightseeing and showing off some of Torry's beauty. Yes, I'm going with you." She had taken my hand in hers as she spoke, and now I got another nice little squeeze as she finished. I enjoyed that, but apparently, she had also said something to the others by way of her mind, and it seemed that I was the only one at the table not aware we were now to be considered a couple.

I was slightly embarrassed, but thrilled as well, and needed to bring things back to my level. "If this is an example of a meal on Torry, I may never leave this little planet. I haven't been able to express myself properly as far as the beauty of this place goes, and I'll never do justice to the food. This is just plain old fashioned good." Riba's raw sense of humor ended the conversation.

"You can't leave until we let you, Tom. You don't know how yet."

Chapter Six

Dinner was coming to a close and my mind was full of Wyoming, Montana, and Nevada, full of the days when I had a family, full of what I wanted almost as much as I wanted to know about the old people. Here was a wonderful and loving family of four having two men over to join them for dinner, not unlike so many dinners I have had with married friends over the years. I miss my family, I miss the little jokes passing back and forth, the gentle reminders about manners and courtesy, the love that goes into a family dinner, every night.

Maybe I'm not the crusty old bachelor I try to be, maybe I'm just a big softy, a creampuff filled with gooey stuff that runs out my eyes every time I think of family. I want a family, that I know, but I haven't been in a position to create one. Almost, that one time, but that sure as hell didn't happen. I can almost see myself in Rohn-Da's seat, lovely children, friends over to share, and I'm going to be a blubbering mass of goo myself if I don't stop this.

"Let me help with the dishes, Tanda. Being an old bachelor I'm pretty good at clearing the table and cleaning up the dinner mess. It's the least I can do as a guest in your wonderful home." There was a quizzical look across her face. She turned to Riba, then to Rohn-Da, and it was younger daughter Tetta who came to her rescue.

"Tom, is that another human thing?" She was smiling, but she also was as curious as her mother. "If we want to clean up after dinner, we just let it happen. Here, watch." She closed her eyes, something I hadn't seen any of the others do when working their mind magic, and the dishes and food moved from view. "I'm not as good at it as mama or Cor-ah, but I am getting better." Tetta's smile was just as bright and full of good humor as her older sister's, but I had questions running through my mind now, probably equal to hers about me wanting to help.

Cor-ah would have simply done the job. Tanda moved things while holding conversations, and Riba moved us through some 8,000 years of existence without even giving a nod. Why did Tetta have to close her eyes to accomplish this feat? I've been under the impression that everyone connected with this universal council was about the same, particularly in their ability to move through space and time, to move objects about, to be able to control so much of their personal space, environment.

All the group except Tetta was looking at me. I'm getting kind of used to this even though on Earth it would be almost bad manners. It was Cor-ah who spoke up, that flashing smile missing this time. "Not all of our people are born with the same abilities as others, Tom." She glanced over at Tetta who was putting the final touches to clearing the table, oblivious to what was going on. Tetta does not have the mind power of the rest of her family. The words screamed into my head before I could do anything about them.

Cor-ah took my hand and led me out into the garden, actually led me, there is no other way to explain what she was doing. We moved out across a beautifully landscaped area that would have been called a back yard at home, sat down on a bench and she looked deep into my eyes. "I like you very much, Tom. Very much, but I don't understand you. Maybe it is the differences between humans and us, but to let your mind say the things it did inside the house is not something Torrians do. You could have humiliated and embarrassed poor little Tetta very much. She was born slightly slow, Tom, but it isn't something we discuss in front of her."

I felt horrible. I know I could have humiliated the girl without even knowing it, I know this now. I looked up into the sky, into a panorama of billions of stars, and for the first time began to understand the differences in people. I have been trying to create a picture in which we are more alike than different. Now, I need to bring myself by to reality and remember where I am. I can't see a single group of stars that I recognize, I'm with a beautiful lady that I must remember is not a human from earth no matter how much I want her to be.

"Cor-ah, as humans we think problems through without voicing the questions or the answers until we know what we're talking about. At least, that's what we tell ourselves we do. I would never purposely hurt anyone, particularly a member of your family. I must go in and apologize." I've committed a serious breach of courtesy and manners and I must make it right. If not for Tetta, if not for me, if only because it's the right thing to do, I must do this. Cor-ah took my hand and stopped me from standing up and leaving the yard. Her eyes still sparkled, she was smiling, but something has changed now in what was a beginning to a relationship.

"No, you just sit here with me for a few more minutes. There is much we need to talk about and this is a good time to do it." She settled herself into the contours of the bench, folded my hand firmly around hers and squeezed it tight. As Tanda had said earlier, the women of Torry are the stronger sex and Cor-ah has taken control. This is her discussion and I'm either the target or the subject depending on how this turns out. Her eyes were so bright, so full of life and fun and knowledge, and she looked at me like a scolding aunt might. I shrank into the bench, tightened my grip on her hand, I wasn't letting go of that hand, and prepared to have my ass chewed out.

The tinkle of laughter caught me completely off stride. "I have no intentions of biting your ass, Tom." It was my turn to laugh, and the picture that came into my head made her laugh even more. Thank God, she isn't going to send me home in shame.

"I'm going to ask something very special of you, and it may even be something that you have no control over, but when you are with all of us, try to remember that we hear every word you are saying. You think you're just thinking these things, but to us, you are speaking, and it's just a lucky thing that this time no one got hurt. Tetta does not have the mind that the rest of us have. It's a shame, and there are a few others like her on Torry, but she just isn't like the rest of us."

"On Earth, we also have people with mental problems, and unfortunately some people take advantage of them or make fun of them. I don't ever want to be put in that class, Cor-ah. I would never hurt someone, physically or psychologically. Tetta is your sister and I would rather be whipped or be sent home in disgrace than hurt her. Please believe me." I wanted to get on my knees and beg. I would have too if she hadn't simply reached over and kissed me.

I mean that sincerely, she kissed me. "We're going to be very close friends, dear Tom, and that's why we're out here in the garden. We can talk out here, we can discuss our differences and no one can hear us. I'm positive you did not intend to hurt dear little Tetta and that's why I got you out of there so fast.

"Your mind is delicious and you can be very wry on the one hand and very deep and philosophical on another, but I know you wouldn't hurt Tetta or anyone else in my family. We work very hard to protect our little girl and I'm just glad she didn't pick up on anything you were saying."

All my life I have been prey to beautiful women. I melt into puddles when they look at me, my knees simply won't hold me up when they make simple little advances or create tender moments, and right now if I had to stand up I would fall flat on my face. I almost ruined what is becoming the most wonderful possibility ever in my life. I almost embarrassed the little sister of a woman that just gave me a serious tongue lashing on the one hand and a gentle loving kiss on the other.

"Cor-ah, this can't be real. I must be mad. You told me that you have already told your family that we are to be considered a couple, I almost publicly humiliated your little sister, I'm falling in love without question, and I'm on a planet in a galaxy that I have never heard of. And tomorrow we are to begin an investigation into the possibility of our universe being under siege. This cannot possibly be." That horrible old woman in the white dress, the one carrying the cattle prod must be just steps away.

"You're not mad, Tom. Riba told us you are a respected member of the human race, that people read things you write. I'm not completely sure what that means, but for Riba to feel strongly about you is good enough for me. My papa loves you dearly and he told me he is looking forward to going to Earth with you." She smiled and said, "He wants to drink your beer. Listen Mr. Human Tom, my papa isn't the kind of man that hangs out with crazy people." She laughed out loud when she said that and grabbed me again, and again planted a wonderful kiss on my welcoming chops.

"You children better come in now. It's up early and off tomorrow for us." Rohn-Da was standing in the backdoor of the cylindrical house. He's not angry with me, I can tell that and Cor-ah still has me in a nice hug, so even though I feel terrible about what I have done, apparently no one was seriously hurt. Thank God. Or maybe that should be, thank Clotero. I am confused.

Cor-ah showed me to my room, up two flights, above where Riba, Rohn-Da and I had our get together, and down a short hallway. "That's my room there," she said, "and this is yours." She closed the door and I could see very little difference between this bedroom and one I might find on Earth, with one exception. The walls of course followed the design of the cylindrical building.

"We're going to have a long and happy relationship my new friend." She had my hand again, squeezing it, threading her tapered fingers into mine, and using those magnificent eyes to drown me in warmth. Several times in the past few hours, I've had little dreams of awakening to those eyes devouring me. It's a grand thought. Cor-ah continued talking even though I'm sure she just caught what I was thinking.

"I want you to know what I feel. I have a strong attraction for you, my family knows this, and I also want you to know that I understand your attraction for me. This is good, and I'm looking forward to what will happen. Now, a simple hug, a gentle kiss, and we'll start our new adventure in the morning. Sleep well, Tom."

I still have those feelings that this can't be, that it's a mad mind playing evil jokes on me, but I want it to be real. I want it to be real. "Tom, your mind talk is distracting sometimes. You're not insane, really. Riba said you might say something like this, but this is very real, and what we're doing is very real.

"Now, kiss me, human Tom, kiss me, and then get some rest." My heart was racing, pounding. There isn't a single NASCAR driver that could keep up with my heart. John Glenn at break-away speed would be passed if my heart had wings. I had a good sweat beading on my forehead. I was in heaven. I'm not exactly movie star handsome, by anyone's imaginative stretch, but I've had some attractive women enjoy my company in the past. No one like Cor-ah. We kissed, gently as she asked, and she slipped out the door.

Sleep was a long time coming. One should be calm for sleep to come, and calm is not in my vocabulary right now. First, where am I? Yes, on Torry, but where the hell is Torry? I'm not even familiar with the many galaxies and planetary systems in the Milky Way, and now I find myself

81

on some incredible journey to galaxies and planets involved in a Universal Council.

Some little old Aztec guy shows up on an archaeological jaunt of mine, and I'm involved in solving a universal mystery? Some guys from hell are screwing women all over the universe in order to bring chaos?

Now, I'm falling in love with a woman I just met this afternoon? Afternoon? Of what day? How long have I been gone? Where the hell am I? I want to believe, I really do want to believe, but if I told this story to my mother, she would ask what I had been drinking. Another little thought: If this is true, and if we are successful in stopping the nether-people, and if I'm returned to Earth, will I be sane?

All these questions are starting to really bug me, bouncing around the head bone. Why haven't I felt cold or hot? Why haven't I been uncomfortable in any way? I'm not even wearing my own clothing. I was dressed as the Council was when we met, and now, I'm dressed as a Torrian, but don't remember changing. Too many questions, not enough answers.

I slipped out of bed and walked to the window. There isn't a single constellation I can recognize. I'm so far away from my own solar system that stars in the sky form different patterns. At some point, I must have answers.

A gentle tap at the door brought gentle words from Riba. "Let it rest now, Tom." I snickered to myself, climbed back in bed, and was fast asleep immediately, and yet, within minutes, it was morning. Cor-ah was shaking me and I awoke to a grand Torrian smile coupled with those sparkling eyes I dreamed about. Her hair, cascading brilliant red hair swirled around her finely sculpted face. I awoke in heaven.

"Did you know your mind is just as active when you're asleep as when you're awake? How do you rest,

Tom? My heavens, I'd be worn out all the time." That smile followed her face right down to mine, as she kissed my forehead.

"Good morning. Will I get awakened like this often?" She sat on the edge of the bed while I tried to collect myself. "Is everyone else already up?"

"Another one of our differences, Tom. We can tell ourselves when to wake up. I guess humans don't do that. It will be fun teaching you all these things. The shower's right over there and breakfast will be ready when you come downstairs." Another little kiss on the forehead and she was gone, and I still had questions. Maybe that's the reason for my being here, to ask questions.

The Universal Council seemed to be more interested in the nether people as entities than the questions of why they came, what they might want, whether they were sent as agents of destruction, all the questions a human government agency might ask. I seem to be the only one asking questions, and when I do, those around me respond as if the thoughts had never entered their minds. Tene was surprised at my questions when we were with the Yeti, and yet, as soon as I formed the questions they seemed to make sense to him.

I have the feeling that no one from any of the other galaxies has actually met, seen, or personally had contact with one of these nether people, that the only thing that seems to be known is that there are people on Earth that are different from other subspecies. This isn't the strongest argument I've ever heard to justify knowledge of an invasion. From what I've seen there is no question that those of us on Earth are different from the other subspecies, but what has led these Quarians to suppose it is an invasion from a parallel universe?

I just voiced my real question. It is the Quarians alone that are behind this investigation and the answer to why will answer the entire problem. Not one of the other subspecies has voiced a question such as why there is an invasion or why they believe there is an invasion. Only the Quarians.

Something I've noticed that I ask more questions than Riba or Rohn-Da. Riba has said the Quarians are a little bit arrogant, I wonder if it extends to feeling they don't have to ask questions? Would their ego extend to them thinking they don't need to ask questions? That would be about as egotistical as one could get. These are thoughts I must pursue. These are the differences and it is the differences that might lead us to the nether people if nether people actually exist. It is also the differences that will allow me to understand some of these people and their ways. Riba is not like Rohn-Da in any way and yet the Torrian subspecies was created by Riba's species. Rohn-Da and I are far more alike than Riba and I. I must work on this.

My studies of the old people will not be put aside by all this. I will continue to pursue my own selfish agenda of learning about the people that came before us, and now that I am with people that can move through periods of time, I will be able to create a true history of the ancient civilizations. At the same time, I can learn when and why these so called nether people have come to this universe. I find it fascinating that of all the people I've met on this journey, none seem the least bit curious of their past.

Rohn-Da said that young people moved from this tropical island Toland to better themselves and to get jobs, and yet he said he didn't understand the concept of cities and industry. There are great gaps in what I think I'm seeing and hearing and what I'm being told. I don't get involved in conspiracy theories but if I did, I might just start thinking I'm in the middle of one. These Quarians are so much different than Torrians, and humans, and it seems that only Quarians make the rules. There's something to give some thought to. I won't speculate on conspiracy, but

I sure would like to know how Rohn-Da, Riba, Cor-ah, and everyone else I've met think without benefit of questions.

Fourth graders might groan and grumble about learning names and dates, but the history of the Earth is so rich in so many ways.   Combine exciting history with exceptional writing, and I find myself tucked into my little rocker-recliner for hours at a time.   These people don't have books, at least I haven't seen a single book, don't ask the questions that would lead to a pathway of investigation, and yet they can move through time and space at will, talk to each other within their minds only, and consider humans baffling.   This entire situation has me baffled for sure.

Breakfast was some Torrian fruit, very sweet, and a hot drink that put double caffeine mocha to shame.   "What is this?"

"We call it mako, Tom.   We like to say it will put hair on your back."   Rohn-Da wasn't kidding, either. "Drink up, the shuttle leaves in about an hour.   I've made reservations, and our bags already have some vacation stuff in them.   Tropical clothing and what not.   We'll be right on the equator and surrounded by the sea, so it'll be damned hot and muggy."   I'd never heard one of my new universal friends use a swear word before, but it fit, coming from Rohn-Da.   I can't picture little Riba saying anything like that.

"What should we do first?"   The roly-poly Torrian was ready for vacation, I think, and I got the feeling he enjoyed planning adventures.

Riba gave him his answer, one he hoped to hear. "Let's just be on vacation.   We'll walk around and look at the sights.   If Tom and Cor-ah do some sightseeing and you and I do other tourist things, we just might make contact." Cor-ah nodded her agreement, and again, I was glad she was going along.

"Tom, you said Qadroth thought your mind clutter would frustrate these nether people.   More than it does us?"

I didn't have time to answer through the merriment, but Riba did.

"The way Qadroth explained it, these people's minds aren't as quick as ours, and the clutter from Tom's would really be a frustration. But let's remember the other things. There might be larger clues, things like taking pleasure in making someone uncomfortable, hurting somebody, having something bad or evil appear as good or entertaining for them. These are more apt to give them away than just frustration at being around Tom. Sorry, Tom."

"I'm getting used to it, Riba. We have to remember that in their universe, everything is reversed from ours. I think the key things to watch for are selfishness and arrogance. I haven't seen any unseemly amounts of either in the short travels I've had through our universe. They are prevalent on Earth, and I'm sure will be dominant with them." As I said the last couple of words, I found we had traveled to what Rohn-Da called the shuttle station. I'll never get used to it, I guess. How the hell do they do it? Or, I guess through their own mind talk everyone knows it's about to happen. They need to warn me.

"You know, Riba, if we moved like this on Earth, sure as hell we'd land on top of somebody and start a massive problem. We have what's commonly called road rage at home, and obscene gestures dominate traffic on major highways. With this form of transportation, I can't imagine how many middle fingers we'd see during morning commute." I guess I was the only one of the four of us who thought what I said was even slightly funny. Cor-ah gave me a look of frustration, Rohn-Da was trying to smile as if he understood, but it was obvious, he didn't have a clue as to what I was talking about.

I just realized that I have spoken often of Earth, Rohn-Da and his family speak often and warmly of Torry, but Riba never speaks of his home world. I wonder if that is another Quarian difference or just another part of their ego.

Our shuttle station did not resemble a bus or train station on Earth in any way. Well, it had floors, ceiling, walls, rounded of course, but other than that, just what appeared to be a number of small compartments along the walls, compartments that might hold as many as six or eight people. No clerks selling tickets, no platform where one might board a vehicle, just the compartments along the walls.

Just as at Rohn-Da's house, the colors were magnificent with reds and blues, greens and yellows, all well blended into myriad fusions of color and movement. One thing the Torrians have is a magnificent sense of art, color, and style. The shuttle station was friendly and warm and that is sure more than I can say about most bus and train stations back home.

"Okay one other question. If we can travel as we just did, why do we need to come to a shuttle station in order to go to Toland?"

Cor-ah answered quickly. "Toland only has room for so many people, only has accommodations for so many, and so we must make prior arrangements to go there. We don't need permission to travel, we need permission to stay." There must be travel agents even on Torry. I wanted to continue this conversation but apparently the three of them had already made our plans. If nothing else comes of this quest of mine, I will learn how to mind talk as they do and I will figure out some way to learn how to move through time and space. "Come on, Tom. Let's not be late for our first day together." That quickened my pace a bit.

We walked over to what looked like a telephone booth, large enough however, for all of us fit in. Rohn-Da waited till we were all in, closed the door, inserted a token of some kind, and when he opened the door, we were standing just off the beach alongside a tropical lagoon, waves gently lapping at an azure sand, a perfumed breeze wafting through our midst, and surrounded by more of Torry's beautiful flora.

I can't begin to describe either the plants, or the feeling of all at once being on a tropical isle. The air felt heavy and wet but not uncomfortable, and my first reaction was to take a swim. I fought that off, but found I had to walk over to one plant and take a look. "That's called a clatta-clatta bush, Tom." It was tall, with multiple leaves coming from a central stem or trunk, purple in color, and with bright orange fruit seeming to drip as from a faucet from the stem. Cor-ah continued.

"The fruit is the sweetest on Torry. One will keep you full of energy all day. We'll have one for breakfast in the morning, if you like." I had my hands on one, and it was surprisingly heavy, with a distinctive and sweet fragrance.

Rohn-Da pointed to a group of small cylindrical buildings just off the beach. "Our rooms, folks. Those two on the left are for Riba and me, and that other one is for you and Cor-ah."

"Uh, whoa." That's as far as I got.

"That's the way Cor-ah wants it, Tom. Now, Riba, let's you and me get settled. We'll all meet back here for dinner." The two went off as without a care in the world, just a couple of friends enjoying a tropical vacation, leaving me standing with my teeth in my mouth. For the first time I noticed that we were all dressed in tropical attire. They've done it again. I'm wearing a light sleeveless pull over type shirt, nicely tailored shorts, and sandals. Cor-ah is stunning in a blazing green tank top that sets her hair on fire and shorts similar to mine. Who made the decision to pick these particular outfits? Cor-ah just shook her head, looked me up and down, smiled and continued talking.

"Tonight, Tom, I'll introduce you to the pleasures of a Torrian woman, but right now, my friend, we have some work to do. I've never been here, so let's first find a map and take a tour of some of the sights, shall we? Your mind is wicked, Tom, but fun." She knew exactly what I was thinking and it didn't have anything to do with finding tourist sights on Toland.

"You must teach me this mind reading you all seem to do with such ease. It's not fair when you and everyone around me know what I'm thinking, and I don't have a clue what you're thinking." There went my mind again, flowing off in another direction, but in line with our work.

"You know my little Torrian bombshell, this may be how we'll find these nether-people. Qadroth thought my mind talk would drive them nuts, but if it is the other way around, that wouldn't work. Qadroth is very wrong in this instance, pretty lady. Since it is probably one of their dominant genes that hasn't allowed us humans to be able to mind talk and not develop as most of the others in this universe have, maybe if we find someone suspicious, and I'm thinking strange thoughts and they aren't picking up on them, you'll be able to recognize this.

"Cor-ah, sweet Cor-ah, I have to have some hinges loose somewhere. I mean all of this is making sense to me. I'm an intelligent fellow, at least by earth standards, and I've always had this quest for truth, it isn't logical to think that all at once, I've just gone bonkers, gone tits up as we say on Earth.

"I'm here, with you, trying to solve some inter-universal mystery, and my mind is telling me, this really is reality. Is this real? Am I really here, with you? God, Cor-ah, help me."

She put her arms around me and planted a kiss that wobbled my knees and straightened my hair. It was not the gentle kiss I got last night, and I hope there are lots more like it. "Poor Tom. I know how this must be taxing, but it is reality. You must know now, I really do exist. This planet exists.   These nether people exist, and they are planning to destroy our universe.

"You know something else, my human friend. You kiss nice." Okay, at least for the time being, I'm going to set aside my fears of mental collapse, particularly if it means I get more of those kisses, and other things that were promised.

"Quit that, Tom." Her smile held the same evil thoughts as my mind, and she let her eyes speak in their own language, with verbs and things that said all that needed to be said. "Over there, that kiosk looks like an information center of some kind. Let's get a map and see where we're going. And no funny stuff, buster." I'm still afraid of saying certain things, but as Riba always points out, I can't control what goes through my mind. She's looking so deep in my eyes, what is she thinking? What's going on in that wonderful head? On Earth, I would be thinking these same thoughts, but not worried that they would be known. This is going to take some serious changing on my part. Now, the look is replaced by one of exasperation, and I know exactly what that means. "Just shut up, Tom."

"You may be right about how the mind talk will affect a nether person. We know for a fact how it affects us, daddy's eyes actually shut some when you really get rambling around in your mind, and it can hurt just a bit. But, as you say, humans don't have the ability to hold mind conversations, and if that is because of nether genes, it will give us an advantage.

"You asked before why haven't you heard questions from any of us, and now I'm asking, too. This is something that you picked up on immediately, yet, apparently, no one from any of the other galaxies has given a thought to. There really are big differences between us, Tom, and they may hold the answers we're looking for."

This island paradise called, Toland is actually three islands, one totally uninhabited, and the other two dedicated to tourism, with just a small area set aside for food production, agriculture.   Cor-ah and I decide that would be a logical place to start since the idea, we think, is for these nether-people to begin their insemination on this planet in these islands. If there is an industry of some kind, it would give them a reason for living in the area.   Not being familiar with the way Torrians talk and move about with their minds would not allow them to hold a permanent job in the tourism industry, but an agricultural job would not be something that would contribute to their being found out.

"I can't get over this ability to move from place to place simply with the mind. How did we just do this, Cor-ah?   One minute we're standing next to a tourist center, next, we're in the middle of a little village, miles away. You must take the time to explain, please, or I promise, I will go crazy."   The little giggles were genuine, but the answer held no promise. We are standing in a little village even though Rohn-Da has no idea of what a village might be.

"In time, Tom. In time. Let's go over to that little restaurant and get something to eat. I would guess it's kind of a meeting place, a social center, and we might pick up something of interest.   Also, just give a little tap or two with your fingers if you want me to pay attention to what you're thinking. That way, I won't give it away. And no dirty stuff either. You're a bad man, Tom." Her humor thrilled me,   and   it   meant   also   that   she   trusted   me completely.   Earth women could learn something from Cor-ah.

We're in a little village I just remembered and Rohn-Da had given me the impression that he didn't know what I was talking about when we discussed cities and industrial areas. We're in an agricultural industrial area, in a village. "Cor-ah, what do you call this grouping of buildings associated with the agricultural complex?" Maybe some of my confusion has to do with something as simple as semantics.

"On the mainland we would call it a sardiff, where people make a living. I'm not sure here, but it would be close to that."

Semantics or whatever, one little mystery cleared up. Sardiff. Thousands more questions to go. As much as I'm glad that I'm alone with Cor-ah right now, I wish, too, that Rohn-Da and the rest of that family were here too. Her family, if it were an Earth family, would be a delight to know. Such love, warmth, and humor in abundance. They would be friends anywhere in the universe. Their love for Tetta is as sincere as it is possible to be and their immediate defense of her was wonderful. I'm still embarrassed by my actions last night. Damned and stupid is the best way to describe me right now.

See? I can accept that I'm here, that is, on Torry. Meeting Rohn-Da, Tanda, Cor-ah, and her sister Tetta makes me think so much of my own family, gone so many years. Dinner last night could have been at the old Iowa farm, or even on the ranch when dad worked in Wyoming. Amazing, that from a boy in Wyoming, I'm a man on Torry, and I can't ever stop thinking of my family. Dad would have immediately fit right in with this bunch.

Dad would have challenged Riba to arm wrestle and mom would have been in the kitchen learning how to cook pigglies, whatever the hell they are. Little Dan, God I miss him the most, I think, he would have been sitting on Tanda's lap telling stories about fishing and chasing rabbits and cutting school. All of them were killed in an instant when that truck missed the turn and wiped out the Buick. I was supposed to be with them for the Christmas holidays, but missed my plane because of a snowstorm, and they were heading back to the ranch after finding out I wasn't on my flight.

God, I do miss them, and maybe this is a trick of my mind, but I love my new family, all different, all loving and a real family. I wonder if I'll screw up and call Rohn-Da dad or Tanda mom. I know I'd like to. They love each other just as mom and dad did, and like them, they're good friends to boot. Here comes the goo.

I guess that's how I remember mom and dad, as best friends, walking fence lines, fishing on weekend camping trips, even dancing at the Grange Hall on weekends. Dad never raised his voice despite how much trouble little Dan and I caused. A look, never even a scowl, just a look, and we would be reprimanded as if by way of a paddle.

Mom now, that's different. She had a temper and I don't think she ever tried to control it. If things weren't going right, mom would yell, pound her little fist, stomp around the house, and dad would head for the barn. "It's the only safe place to be, boys, the barn is my salvation." Within minutes mom would calm down, dad would come back to the house, and whatever the crisis had been would be considered resolved. I don't ever remember them yelling at each other, but inanimate objects were thoroughly raked over the coals. "Stupid lamp!" "Damn table!" "Get out of the way, cat!"

I haven't seen what might be called a temper in my new family, but I know I came mighty close last night. Cor-ah was upset, and I was the cause, but if that's as close to a temper, then these people really are special. I remember mom spending more than five minutes chewing out a rolling pin because her piecrust didn't turn out exactly as she wanted. Dad and Rohn-Da would be friends, that is a given, but I don't know if mom and Tanda would make it. Mom could lose her temper and within moments, be loving

93

and smiling and whatever got her started would be forgotten.

It's been a long time since I've had these thoughts, remembering all the good times and that one horrible time. We were a close family and shared so much love just as these wonderful Torrians seem to do. Dad was a worker, strong as a bull and not afraid of man or beast. He wrestled calves and full-grown bulls as well, rode the meanest horses and broke them to ride with soft words and gentle touches, never the whip. I always thought he would be disappointed that I turned out to be a writer and not a cowboy or woodcutter, but he wasn't. He was proud as hell of what I did, and often would tell his friends about his son, the writer.

He had some of the same thoughts about the ancient people on earth that I have but never had the desire to investigate their history. He was always pleasantly amazed when he came across some of the ancient writing or some old encampment area. I took him along on many of my earliest searches. God, would he love to be here with me right now.

Maybe that's the point of this madness, to bring me back to reality, make me remember my own wonderful family and past life. Maybe there aren't any nether people or isn't any Universal Council. What about Cor-ah? What about Rohn-Da and Riba? What about those thoughts I just had about Cor-ah's sister, Tetta?

I have to remember to talk to Cor-ah about Tetta, a sister in looks but not personality. Tetta seems kind of cold and withdrawn. Just a family difference, I suppose. What if it was more than that? What if the nether people arrived here several years ago, maybe even generations ago, and began the invasion from these islands?

But that's a horrible thought. It could mean that Tanda has been here before and may have had relations with a nether. I can't believe I'm thinking this, but Tetta is so very much different, and she did not pick up on my thoughts the same way the rest of the family did.

Again, Cor-ah is looking deep into my eyes. "You may have something there, hot shot. Tetta is very different from the rest of the family, as you know. She doesn't have the strength in her mind like the rest of us. Oh, dear. The implications of this are frightening, Tom. This could very well mean that my mother had relations with another man, possibly a nether person, fifteen years ago when they were here on vacation. This is where Tetta was conceived, Tom.

"You may not have the ability to talk with your mind as we do, but your powers of deduction are far stronger. This is very disturbing."

These thoughts are tearing me apart. I love my new family and now look what I'm thinking about them. "It doesn't have to mean that, Cor-ah. It may just be that Tetta isn't as fully developed as most Torrians. All humans are not born with equal intelligence levels or physical functions, and I would imagine it's the same here. I certainly didn't mean to imply that your mother was unfaithful to your father." Damn my mind, damn it to hell, if this is what happens. Shame on me, and I hope Cor-ah understands there wasn't anything personal in my thoughts.

"That isn't the problem, Tom. Torrian women can have as many lovers as they wish, but just one husband. But it is rare for one to allow herself to get pregnant by someone other than her husband. If Tetta is from nether seed, I wonder if my mother even knows that?" We stopped our chatter as we approached the restaurant, actually, just a cafe, and entered. There were a few workers at a counter, and one man, sitting alone in a booth. We walked toward an open booth, and that man's eyes pulled a human's trick of all but undressing Cor-ah. He also gave me a full going over.

I gave a look back and he quickly looked away. I hadn't any thoughts in my head, but Cor-ah picked up and gave a look toward the man as well. "We got quite a looky-look there." Cor-ah laughed out loud at that comment as we took our seats.

"Looky-look. That's a hell of a description. Humans have some funny expressions, but they all mean something. Looky-look. I'm going to spring that on papa. No, it would be more fun to use it on Riba.

"But you're right. He gave me the impression he wanted to come over and say something. Like he knew us."

"You. I bet he thinks he knows you. You look so much like your mother, I wonder if we could be lucky enough to bump right into a nether person? Cor-ah, if he gets his courage up, let's let him join us or whatever, or let's see if we can't bring it about." She handed me a menu, and I glanced at it and handed it right back. That was a trick from my dad when he didn't have any idea what he wanted to eat. In my case, I had no idea what I was looking at.

"You order, dear heart. I don't have any idea what any of these names mean. For all I know, roqua might be toad's liver or something." Her nose crinkled up at that, and she was smiling delightfully, but out of the side of her eyes.

"I don't know what a toad is, Tom, but roqua is really good. I'll order us some. Don't look, but that man is about to come over here. I'll take the lead, but you can jump in any time. That would be the Torrian way." I watched the guy get up through a reflection in the window, and he was trying to be casual as he walked toward us. I couldn't read anything in his face; anger, guilt, or just being curious. He looked right at Cor-ah when he got to the table, and by golly, he was smiling.

Of course, he was smiling, he was about to start a conversation with a beautiful young woman. On Earth, an approach as forward as this could net a guy a shiner or broken nose, but I had the feeling on Torry, it was acceptable. "Hello.   I couldn't help noticing when you came in.   We don't get too many tourists on this side of the island.   Are you looking for someone or something special? Maybe I can help."

That's a straight forward approach, nothing clandestine or out of line.   I tried to read anything in his words, his face, but everything appeared genuine, honest. His face and hands were that of a man who spent hours working outdoors. He was tanned and creased from the weather, his hair tousled, but not unkempt or unclean.   He wore his clothes as if he was comfortable in them, and they were a working man's clothes, rugged, but not dirty or ragged.   His appearance and manner were genuine and honest, I thought.   All the time I was looking at him, smiling back and forth between the man and Cor-ah, I was tapping my fingers lightly on the table.

"Hi.   We're not really tourists.   We've been doing some research on tropical farming for the Universal Council, and hoped we would be able to meet someone who could give us a good tour of some of the agricultural areas around here.

"My name is Cor-ah, and this is Tom.   Tom is from the Marq system and hopes to bring some of our ideas to his home planet.   Are you associated with one of the aggie systems here?"

Oh, she's good.   I know now that he isn't reading my thoughts at all and is really concentrating on her.   I'm going to let it all hang out here for a minute, give him a real blast of an uncontrolled human mind and see what happens.

In fact, just thinking about it, and my thoughts turn to Riba and how he squirms when I start thinking too much, and how the Council all held their heads, and how in the hell did I get here?   This can't possibly be real, sitting in a cafe, nuttier than a fruitcake, in never-never land as far as my used-to-be mind goes.

Cor-ah's eyes have closed and I'm afraid I'm hurting her. Shut it off, Tom. She smiled lightly, and looked at the stranger.

"I would be glad to give you folks a tour. My name is Kantor El, and I operate one of the processing plants here. This is the slow time for growing and processing, so I have a bit of time.

"Cor-ah. That's a charming name. My father has a picture of a beautiful young woman who could be your sister." He laughed right out loud, "Or your mother." Did he mean to imply that Cor-ah's mother might mess around some? That would be the way a nether would think. Hurt someone if the chance presents itself.

Cor-ah pulls off a real blush, and with her eyes averted from mine, she knows she would break up with her sense of humor, she tells Kantor El that we would love a tour. "First, we need to find a place to stay. There's much work to do in our research. Is there a hotel nearby?" My darling little Cor-ah is a pure con, and this nether person is hooked, ready to give away state secrets.

"There's a hotel just across the street." He took out some papers and handed them to her. "The Roqua Pure plant is right over here, and if you'd like, I can meet you in about an hour." If they grow it, Roqua Pure isn't toad's liver, I guess. Cor-ah turned away quickly, but not before I caught the smile.

Arrangements made, we finish lunch and head for the hotel. "Toad's liver. You will tell me what a toad is, some day, won't you?" Things are going well, I'm thinking, and as we enter the room, here we are again, standing on the beach back in Toland City, just outside our little cabin there. I was still closing the door when we left. I'll never get used to it and this time she didn't tell me it was coming to get even about toads and things. Actually, Roqua Pure is very good, I guess similar in its way to potatoes back on Earth. If I had to describe what I had for

98

lunch it would be a platter of chili cheese fried potatoes. That's as close as I'll ever get, and, while it isn't really close, Roqua is not toad's liver.

Riba and Rohn-Da are waiting for us, it seems they knew that fast that we were coming. "This might take some time, but I think Tom has solved part of this problem, and created still another one. A big problem that I don't want to bring up, but I have to." Cor-ah spent the next hour or so explaining what we found.

For a daughter to calmly tell her father that her mother, his wife, may have been messing around with some aliens and gotten herself knocked up would bring the walls and ceilings in on someone on Earth.

"I understand some things, now." Rohn-Da was contemplating what was just said, said by his own daughter, about his wife, and about his youngest daughter. "Tanda and I were in ecstasy while we were here, and you know how we can get. She must have forgotten to protect herself. It does answer so many questions about pretty little Tetta, though, you know, the way she is.

"I wonder if Tanda even knew that she was pregnant by this other man, and not by me? Well, Riba, what do we do now? This Kantor El is expecting these two to be at his processing plant soon."

The similarities between Torrians and Earthlings are many, but it's obvious there are also some big differences. Tanda and Rohn-Da are on vacation, making it with each other often, and Tanda still goes off and has a fling with a field worker? Well, farm owner. Behavior like this would be the making of a soap opera at home. I'm looking at these people as family, but it will take considerable acceptance on my part to really be a part of them.

Cor-ah gave me a gentle little squeeze of the hand again and smiled that smile of hers and I knew deep in my heart these people were my family. Philosophers have always talked about the family of man and I doubt that any would be surprised to learn some of the things I have learned on this visit to Torry. We are one in this universe and despite some little differences, it appears that we really can get along. Now, there's a thought; we can't get along on Earth but we can in the universe. The various problems with being human coupled with the ego and demands of the Quarians, and the gentle approach to life of the Torrians and we have a universal family.

On Earth, much of our history is based on war and on differences that can't be worked out. Diplomacy by another name is how war is defined, but I haven't heard the words war, history, even education now that I think of it. I'm going to have to start taking notes so I'll remember the questions to ask Cor-ah. Torry must be as close to Earth as exists in the universe, and that must have been an open invitation to these nether people.

It does make sense I suppose if I was from the nether world. Go to Earth, as it appears they did, be successful in planting the nether gene, but unsuccessful in being able to spread it about the universe because of the Universal Council's action in not letting Earth into the council.

Torry is so much like Earth, it was easy to come here, and it apparently has been recent. Cor-ah said Tetta's condition isn't a singular event, that there are others on the planet like her. The nethers are here and we need to stop the infestation. But how? What to do about Tetta and those who are like her, carrying the nether genes? Another thought enters my brain about the same time.

What will I bring back to Earth? A knowledge of peoples not much different from ourselves yes, but deeper than that, I will be able to conceptualize how humans on Earth can make themselves as agreeable even as Rohn-Da, or at worst as agreeable as Riba. Are the differences among humans based on these nether genes or is there something else at the heart of our disagreeable nature?

Working with Cor-ah, Riba, and Rohn-Da has made me a different person than I was that day in the Silver Peak desert.

There's that look again. Riba's penetrating eyes actually bore into my soul, I think.   I will know that look until the day I die.   Yes, dear Riba, I'll let it drop for the time being.   Just for you, old friend.   The frown from him was my payoff.   I love it.

Chapter Seven

How different my Earth would be if these nether people had not come so many generations ago and altered our future. We would be working members, yes, partners, in this Universal Council, traveling about the galaxies as we pleased, not having to depend on vehicles of any sort, enjoying the fruits and passions of so many different societies. Is it really the nether induced genes that have made us so different from the rest of the universe? I feel a closeness with those from Torry and, at the same time, recognize similarities between human nature and Quarian nature. These Quarians give me the impression that they could become nasty in a heartbeat, turn on a friend without blinking, which of course is very human like. Yet, I can't help having a strong sense of respect for Qadroth. Riba scares the hell out of me.

There are glaring differences in our cultures and lives that I need to more fully understand, like people don't seem to read or even understand the concept of reading. Rohn-Da not understanding the idea of towns and cities, and yet here I've just come to a small town on the Island of Toland. I'll just take my time and try to understand what these wonderful people are all about.

I am a child in the first learning stages as to how things work in the universe. Actually, I haven't taken my first steps yet. How does Rohn-Da make a living? Why is he on the Council and not Tanda? Where did that food come from last night? What kind of education system exists? Is it universal in nature? One thing I think I do know: There is virtually no inter-breeding among the residents of the various galaxies. Strange then, that Cor-ah is willing to invite me to her bed tonight.

Is Cor-ah a nether? No, not with the power of that mind. When someone like Riba accepts that her mind is strongest, there can be no doubt she is pure Torry. I had to say something before Riba and Rohn-Da made a decision.

"Riba, we may have to do some history juggling here. Instead of meeting with this Kantor El, it may be better to meet with Yannow again, or whoever guards the gates here, and find out when the first nether people arrived.

"Would it be possible then, to simply go back to that time and deny them entrance? It could very well mean that many people who are living on Torry would disappear, history having been compromised. We call it altering the time line in some of Earth's entertainments. Would that bring chaos?"

The three stood looking at each other, obviously in some internal conversation. A few quick glances my way, then back to themselves, and I'm sure debating the pros and cons of what I just said.

It was Cor-ah who spoke first. "Tom, what you have proposed has raised a very serious moral question that cannot be answered by any one of us. By going to the time the nether people entered Torry, and altering history, we would in essence, be killing those who have come from them.

"On the other hand, if we don't, we will be sealing the fate of the universe. When people from each universe merge into one race, there will no longer be opposites, and the two universes will collapse in chaos. This kind of moral dilemma cannot be answered by us. We must have another meeting with the Universal Council and discuss this.

"Tom, you and I will return to the village, meet with Kantor El and learn what we can from him, and Riba, you and papa must insist on a council meeting as soon as possible. Tom and I will join you when we have learned what we can from this nether person." The Torrian female is unquestionably the leader in her realm and there is no doubt that Riba and Rohn-Da will do as she has said. Rohn-Da put his arm around his oldest daughter and hugged her tightly. "It's okay, papa. It's okay." All thoughts were on Tetta and the other children of the nether invasion. Would they die, would they be remembered if history could be altered? Horrible questions. Is this a form of interstellar ethnic cleansing? I would burn in hell before I would condone such action, but the very existence of the universe seems to be at stake. Returning to chaos as these people describe it would end everything we know about life. Yet, how can I even suggest ending the lives of how many young people on Torry?

Riba's eyes were downcast, tears rolling down his cheeks, his head slightly bent, and not willing to look at anyone. "Tom, when we finish this ugly business, I'm going to see to it that you are able to have the same type of mind as the rest of us, but in return, my friend, I'm going to learn your process of deduction. This is the type of ethical question that hasn't been raised in the universe in millions of years. It's this type of philosophical thought that brought about the original breeding, at the will of Clotero." Riba was answering some of my questions, as well. I'm seeing the real person here, not the stern old taskmaster I usually think of as Riba.

On the other hand, here is the Quarian saying "I will see to it that you have the same kind of mind as mine." Do the Quarians really have that kind of power to be able to alter one's mind? He and Qadroth did say they were responsible for taking away the human ability to mind travel. They did say they were responsible for keeping humans out of the Universal Council. Such arrogance.

There's a depth to this man though, that isn't seen from a surface search. He's been to places and talked with beings no one on my planet has ever heard of, and yet he can cry as the deepest feeling human has ever cried. His feelings aren't just for his own people, but for the universal family.   Here we are again, back to the family of man.   That thought of a family of man has been in the philosophical teachings of people on Earth from the time of the Greeks, or maybe even before.   Is it possible that the ancient people, those we think of as cave dwellers were also as philosophical as modern humans?   We know that from the first of what we call civilizations, for instance along the Tigris and Euphrates, there were philosophers, but a written history of those before them doesn't exist.   That will be my job, eh?

In the universe today then, we have those that have inhabited our universe, and those that have invaded from the other side.   From a purely humanitarian point of view, we cannot alter history.   How would we eradicate the nether gene from the human population without literally killing billions of people?   Impossible.   To do so on Torry would be equally criminal.   Not one of these people, on Earth, on Torry, or anywhere else these nethers have gone, is responsible for the issue.   The children of the invasion are pure victims in the largest sense.

On the other hand, we can't ignore what is happening.   Nether genes are being spread through Torry right now, and who is to say they aren't being spread in some of the other galaxies?   Long hours of deep discussion are in our immediate future, I'm thinking.

What Riba just said was, the Quarians were open to conceptual thinking, to dealing with the abstract, at the time of human's inception.   How did the Quarian mind change so radically?   They don't think that way anymore.   Is it their minds that have evolved past ours, or is it a case of an intermingling of nether genes with those of the human, that our minds evolved in different directions?   How much contamination is there in the universe?

Riba's thoughts continued.   "Think what this would mean to your family, Rohn-Da if we altered history, and to how many other thousands, millions of families?   Can we simply kill off a generation of people?   Cor-ah, you and Tom find out what you can, and then join us at Council as soon as possible."   He was stern and determined, and he and Rohn-Da simply vanished from view, and then Cor-ah and I were back in our little hotel room in the village, waiting for a knock on the door from whom we believed would be a man from hell.

"Cor-ah, did you pick up on what I was thinking a couple of minutes ago, about how Quarians and humans have changed over the eons?   We need to discuss this at length, just us, no interference from Riba.   My mind is coming up with questions that we haven't even thought of. We need to do this."

"I can't imagine being able to think as you do, Tom. You call it conceptual, abstract, until I met you I had never heard the words or conceived the idea, but I feel just being around you that I understand.   I agree, we need to sit down and spend several hours discussing this entire mess.   It is a mess, isn't it?"   Her eyes were downcast, there was no smile, and thoughts of little Tetta had to be foremost in her mind.

Nether people, nether world, the underworld, hell. All the stories from mythology and from some of the religions I've read about are real, but in a slightly different concept.   Hell, a nether world?   An opposite universe to balance the physics as conceptualized by Clotero, God? Now, a moral question on a universal scale is in order to protect both universes.   Ours, we consider good, theirs, we consider evil.   Heaven vs. Hell.

Considering all this, why on Earth am I involved, a simple old guy who loves to traipse among history, write stories about the ancient ones, why am I in the middle of a universal mystery that could kill millions, could destroy everything we know, could return billions of years of evolvement to chaos? Why on Earth did someone pick me?

"As scattered as your mind might be, Tom, I love the way you are able to think. Your subspecies may have lost its ability to be one with your mind, but you have gained the ability to mentally grasp a concept. Those of us in the rest of the universe don't have that ability.

"If you can do that simply because of genes from the nether people, I wonder what else they have given the Marquian?" She wanted to smile, wanted to create something positive in the conversation, but I was dark, my mind was black with terrible thoughts. I could hate, and I've never hated before. I believe I could kill a nether if the circumstances were right and I've never killed a man or wanted to. My thoughts on being human were as low as they could get.

"They've given us an oversize ego, a feeling of self-importance far in excess of reality. We can be selfish and cruel with each other, we kill for the thrill of killing, we put our brothers and sisters in bondage, we steal and pillage simply because we feel a need for power. The human being is not a beautiful animal, and I have been made to feel pretty small more than once during these travels with Riba.

"Better than anyone, I understand the morality involved in our current situation, but I can also see what will happen to this beautiful little planet if the nether people are allowed to continue their infestation. Cor-ah, the people of Torry are beautiful and pure, your minds are amazing, and I haven't seen a moment of selfishness or cruelty. I've seen love and warmth. No, this must end now.

"We need to finish our work with this Kantor El and join with Riba and your father. I have a heavy feeling in my heart, Cor-ah, a feeling of dread, and it comes from the only way I can visualize us stopping the nether-people. I would never be able to carry that level of guilt, if it comes to that. I can't imagine being responsible for untold numbers of deaths." Kantor El's arrival stopped my speech, but we are in a much better position as far as dealing with him this time. Cor-ah could understand his thoughts and mine, but he couldn't pick up on either one of ours.

"I made arrangements for a tour of our little agricultural center. Tell me, what kind of research are you doing that would bring you to such a place as Toland? It's hot and humid, miserable conditions in which to work, we can never get enough workers. It seems they all want to head to the mainland somewhere. I often wish we could force people to stay and work the fields and processing plants.

"Well, you didn't come here to listen to me moan and groan, did you? The trip to the fields and plant will take just a moment. Here, let's take hands."

Did you pick up on that, Cor-ah? I was thinking as hard as I could, telling her this dude can't mind travel as she does, but has to have strength from more than one mind to make a trip. That comment about forcing someone to work sounds very much like bondage or slavery. Very Earth like. Let's see if we can entice this jerk to show us that picture he was talking about. I really hope it isn't Tanda. Cor-ah's fingernail in my palm told me, one, she understood everything and two, if I didn't let up she would really give me hell. It was obvious, too, Kantor El didn't understand any of it.

"Show me this picture. Another woman who looks like me? Well, I've heard we all have twins, but I've never given it much thought." Kantor El took the bait immediately, and we went to what appeared to be the supervisor's office, and sure enough, there was a picture of Tanda hanging on the wall.

"You say that's your father standing with that woman? Amazing, isn't it Tom?" It was a horrible affirmation of what we feared. Kantor El seemed pleased showing off the plant, the fields, and most of all, his father's picture. I think he wanted some kind of response from Cor-ah, maybe something about her mother, but she wouldn't give him that kind of pleasure.

Notes taken, 'thank you's given, we held hands, Cor-ah and I, and were immediately back in Toland City. The hand holding was for Kantor El's benefit. "Morals and ethics, lovely lady. How many people have been conceived by these invaders from across the universal border? How many lives will be ruined if we go back to when they arrived and destroy them? Are we in a position to even think about such a thing?" I tried not to cry, but I couldn't stop the tears.

"Oh, Tom, you're such a good man. There must be a way. We'll find a way to stop them, and save those who have become different because of them. We will." Cor-ah was shaking and I think on Earth that would have come from anger and frustration. Her little sister is related to Kantor El and we have been discussing the possibility of ending that child's life, existence. I had been wondering about temper and anger earlier and now I had a partial answer. This lady has a temper and keeps it under control. I don't think I want to be around if she loses her temper.

I held her tight, trying my best to control my emotions. "It will take a brilliant mind, pretty lady. Strong and brilliant to sort this out, to come up with logical and ethical answers. To save the universe do we have the right to kill people? My reaction is no, we don't have that right, but if we don't stop the infestation, how will we stop further breeding, stop further infestation. If we don't stop them, aren't we killing all life in the universe?

"It might be possible to isolate those conceived from nether people, but another dilemma. How do we find out who those might be? We're surmising Tetta is the daughter of a nether person, but it's still just conjecture on our part.   How many others are there, and how will we know who they are?"

"Your powers of conjecture are so much better than mine, Tom.   Let's rest for a while, I'm very tired from all this.   Let's go inside our cabin and rest, then we'll join with Riba and papa."

Our room would have been a typical motel or hotel room on Earth with the exception of the cylindrical walls, and Cor-ah shucked her clothing the minute we entered.

I couldn't move, just stood there staring at Venus, Aphrodite, Cor-ah.

"Come on my new human friend, it's time you learned about some Torry traditions.   I'm looking forward to our relationship, Tom.   I'll teach you some things, and then, you teach me some things.   Earth things.   Isn't it wonderful the way we're built?"

I couldn't speak, couldn't think, just stood there.

"Take your clothes off, hot shot, this is our time, now."

We made love in many ways, in many positions, in passion, in thought, in bed, on the carpet, in the shower. One of the most interesting things to happen was making love using just our minds.

"Don't touch, just think about touching.   Stroke, taste, feel, but only with your mind, your delicious and evil Earth mind.   Make my blood boil, Tom, just with your mind."

It was an incredible experience, because for the first time I was able to feel the strength of her mind.   She also stroked, tasted, felt, and bedeviled, and only with her mind.

Hours of pleasure and I was the one who was worn out.   "What happened to that idea of a rest?   Of a nap?   Is this what you call resting for a few minutes?   Cor-ah, I'm exhausted.   Satisfied, but exhausted."   Another sunrise of a smile, and a prod to get up and dressed, and I knew there wouldn't be any nap soon.

"Riba never came right out and said so, and the reactions of your parents belie what I'm about to say, but I was led to believe there really shouldn't be relations between the subspecies of different galaxies. If that's so, are we breaking some kind of law? Are we criminals now, on top of everything else?"

One can't travel through time and space. I know this. Assuming one could travel through time and space, one human could not expect to stop a universal upheaval of the magnitude we're discussing, a revolution between opposing universes. I can't comprehend the size of our universe. Can't. How can I even think of the concept of twin universes? Twin universes at war.

Now, the preposterous idea that I'm making love with the most beautiful woman I've ever met. She's from another galaxy, a galaxy I've never even heard of, have no idea where it is, and I fear I've broken some universal edict. That big heavy lady in the white coat will have a field day proving I'm a full-blown lunatic.

I just spent hours in passionate physical contact with Cor-ah, and if I ever get back to Earth, and I don't awaken in the loony bin, I'll have some fine tall tales to tell. Now, Cor-ah's eyes, penetrating and smiling, are at the same time giving me hell. Sometimes it's like looking at Riba. Well, a very attractive Riba. "I'm sorry, but really, dear sweet lady, how can any of this be real?"

"Oh, baby, it's real. Look at the dorly pimples all over my body. This is real, Tom, in every sense. While I'm thinking of this, when we make love human style next, you mentioned a snack and then a nap. What happens after the nap?"

"And you say I have a dirty mind. To answer that question, we start over, and then over again. Am I learning to pick up some messages from your mind? I saw the leer in your eyes, but also felt I was getting a message."

"Yeah, you're picking up some of the messages from me because we're working so close. Back to one of your pertinent questions, the Universal Council has made it a point to frown on subspecies inter-breeding. There is a fear of homogenizing some of the genetic make-up of various cultures, but that isn't to say we can't enjoy the pleasures of each other's company. We'll just make sure that I don't get pregnant and, of course, that's completely my worry."

"That's a little different from Earth thinking. Men and women work hard at seeing to it that pregnancy is as planned as possible. Of course, some men are stupid brutes and just don't care, but they are in the minority. Women take birth control pills, use creams and jellies, and other such, while men often will use what we call a condom to keep the sperm from reaching an egg. Many men also have vasectomies which make it nearly impossible for them to procreate."

"That's pretty complicated, my human friend. Here, I simply make it my will that I will not get pregnant. That's it, just a simple little gesture. I think that's what my mother may have forgotten to do in the heat of the situation."

Her smile had a little twinge to it, as if she was thinking how things might have been if none of this had happened. "We have a little time before we have to meet with Riba and your father. I understand how we move about, how the power of your mind is such that we can move through areas on this wonderful little planet, Riba and I did that on Earth as well, but I don't understand how you can move between galaxies and through various periods of time.

"Let's say we have a day or two and I want you to come with me to Earth for a couple of days, what would we have to do?"

"Would you really bring me to Earth, Tom? Can we really go there?"

"Riba and Rohn-Da aren't expecting us for a few days, Cor-ah. Our work is actually over here and I can't think of anything I would rather do than bring you to Earth for a couple of days. You will really enjoy, I promise."

"You are familiar with the areas that are overseen by Yannow and his tribes, Riba has indicated that you and he visited Yannow. Often, they are called areas of great energy, you have told me how the old people on your world moved through them. We move through them the same way. The great ones, Yannow and his tribes oversee all the areas of energy. We will go to one of the areas of great power, an area of universal energy and I'll show you."

Chapter Eight

We had moved that fast, back to the mainland, and were in what appeared to be an area of foothills just above a small town. "Is that the town where you live? I thought Rohn-Da said there weren't any cities or towns as such." I don't know if that was a question or a statement, but Cor-ah ignored me anyway so I'll have to ask again, I guess. Like later. What I'll have to do is define city and town for Cor-ah, and then maybe I'll get the point across. After all, we call population centers by numbers of names, villages, towns, cities, urban centers and on and on. Maybe I didn't get my point across. Cor-ah isn't paying the least bit of attention, except that I can see her glancing at me out of the corner of her flirtatious eyes.

"No, there aren't any areas of strong force near our home. We're a couple of hundred dablos away, near one of the mountain ranges in the countryside. Here, this is what I wanted to show you." There was a pile of rocks, as a cairn might look and we sat down next to it. Cor-ah drew the little peace sign in the dirt and sure enough, a Yeti was sitting with us. "To move through time and space between galaxies we need the help of Yannow's tribes. Members of the Universal Council often have the same powers as the gatekeepers, for instance as does Riba, but for the most part, we need some help."

So, maybe the Quarians do have the ability to give certain powers to certain people. This would be a form of control, I would think, and could be used as a form of punishment as well. Withholding privilege is a punishment well known on Earth, and the Quarians may have a use for it as well. They are becoming more and more perplexing in my mind. There is something missing in my equation, something about the Quarians and humans that is missing.

Cor-ah is giving me a big heavy evil eye right now. It's time for introductions.

"Hello, Tika. This is Tom from Earth in the Marq system."

"Hello Tom, I have heard Yannow say that you have a wonderful mind but are unable to move about as the rest of the subspecies do." He spoke in that same monotone that I remember from Yannow, but he was very pleasant and friendly and I believe he was actually smiling. When I think of Yeti or Bigfoot, or any other anomaly, I tend to put them all in the same dress, but looking at Tika I see many differences between him and Yannow. Tika is actually larger than Yannow and that's saying something. Massive shoulders with long muscular arms, a deep brow with eyes that seem to burn right through me. I do not want him to ever get angry with me.

Now, I have declared that Tika and Yannow are male, and that is just as bad. It is so easy when one is as large as these people are to assume the male sex without so much as a "how do you do?" Stereotyping individuals is again that human trait that leads to such things as bigotry, racism, unwarranted hatred and fear. Are these traits really from the nether world or is this just a human trait that is not beneficial to the race? The Quarian people that I've met often seem as arrogant as any human, yet I have not seen that in the Torry people. Differences are natural on Earth, and it seems in the universe as a whole as well.

Will I have an opportunity to sit with either Tika or Yannow for a period of time and just ask questions? What a thrill that would be. I'm sure there is at least one editor somewhere that would accept such a detailed piece.

"Where are you two off to?" That was certainly casual enough.

"I'm bringing Cor-ah to Earth for a few days, Tika. We need to go to my apartment in Virginia City in my own time, if that's possible?"

"You have learned well, Tom." There we were, standing in the middle of my kitchen in my little apartment in Virginia City, Nevada. Cor-ah took my hand and squeezed it ever so gently as she looked all around taking in everything, dirty dishes in the sink and all. Camping stuff spread around, hiking boots in the middle of the floor, the farthest thing from her ordered home on Torry.

"This is where you live." It was a statement, not a question and she wasn't being the least bit judgmental. "For some reason I just assumed your home would be similar to mine. I've never seen anything like this."

I've not been to any other planet except Torry so I don't know if all the various subspecies build their homes and buildings as cylinders, but from Cor-ah's reaction, I must believe they do. I don't think she has ever seen a squared wall or a room with corners. She immediately walked over to a corner of the room and let her fingers trace the exact corner.

"I've never seen anything like this," she repeated, continuing to run her hand along the wall.

I gave her the complete tour of the apartment. Almost as I did when I first arrived on Torry, she wanted to touch everything. She ran her fingers over lamps and pictures, picked up kitchen utensils, even took a look in the refer, with an amazed look on her face.

When those on Torry simply conjure cooked food out of the clear, something such as a refrigerator must be baffling. She walked over to a large window in the living room. "We're on the second floor of a three story building. This is a very historic old town and this building was built in 1875." She looked questioningly at me and it dawned on me that dates don't mean anything to her.

Of course, they don't, dummy. "We measure time in days and years, and the year 1875 is more than 130 years ago." It still didn't register and I knew enough at this point to just let it go.   My teaching career will have to start with Cor-ah.

"I'll tell you all about that later.   What you're looking at is what we call a town, a city.   It's a place where humans live, have businesses, make a living.   I know that isn't known on Torry, but it is how we live on Earth. She was taking it all in, her eyes wide open, just as mine must have been on Torry.

"There are two businesses on the ground floor of this old building and another apartment on the third floor above us."   She was looking up as I stood next to her, up across the top of the building across the street into the mountain that rises steeply to Virginia City's immediate west.   I remember standing in her driveway looking out across the mountains and valleys of Torry, and I'm seeing a similar expression on her face.   "We're in an area where there are steep mountains but not too much vegetation. Small pine trees and sage brush dominate this area."   From the look on her face it is obvious that she likes what she's seeing but doesn't have the foggiest idea of what I'm talking about.

The kitchen and dining room amazed her, particularly as I explained things and she was aware that so much is done by the mind on Torry and none is done that way here.   Kitchen gadgets were beyond her comprehension.   I pushed the button on an electric can opener and she jumped back about three feet and glared at me when I laughed.   "I enjoyed mako on Torry, let me make us a cup of coffee, and you'll see what I mentioned earlier about them being similar."   That calmed her down, but she was befuddled, all the way this time, by what I was doing to make the coffee.

While the coffee was making I found her in the living room looking out the big windows again, down onto Virginia City's main street.   "What are those things moving around down there, Tom?"   She was pointing at cars and trucks moving along C Street and I remembered there were no such things on the other planets in the Universal Council. Now, I'm just as amazed as she is. As I was moving about on her planet she is moving about here.

"Those are called vehicles, some are cars, some are trucks. That doesn't make much sense to you, I know but it will in just a few minutes. Do you remember Riba telling you that we can't move about with our minds, that we use mechanical devices? Well, those are some of the mechanical devices we use."

I left her by the window and went into the kitchen for coffee. I remember looking out the bedroom window in her home that night, seeing things I had never seen, and now she's fascinated by what's outside that window. "Here, try your first cup of Earth's finest coffee. It's hot, like mako, so just sip."

She took the cup, smelled of it, felt the warmth through the mug, and tasted, very gently, as if maybe I was offering toad's liver. Her eyebrows lifted slightly, "Mmm, this is good. You're right, it is like mako. We have so much in common, Tom, and there are so many differences. I love this. I love you. I love Earth." I thought for a minute she was going to dance or start singing or something. "And you had to make this by putting things together?" She was back to talking about the coffee, and I was beginning to understand more about the Torry mind. Compartmentalized as is Riba's, but with slight variations.

Cor-ah could put things together that always baffled Riba. "Let me show you." We walked into the kitchen and I showed her the process of making a pot of coffee. "Do you want to try?"

She looked at me, and within seconds had a second pot brewing, but she put all the pieces together using just her mind. "You can do that here the same as you would have on Torry? That's just not fair." We laughed, hugged some more. I sneaked a little kiss, and said it's time for her first walk along the streets of an Earth town.

"Will we go in one of those things?" She couldn't remember the names. "Are they dangerous?" She picked up on that problem immediately.

"Darn dangerous, but I'm a good driver. Before we take a drive, let's take a walk and you can better understand why some things on Torry just amaze me." For the first time in how long I wasn't thinking about nether people, wasn't perplexed by the horrible consequences of possibly having to alter Torry's history to the point of actually killing, probably the right word would be eliminating, some of the young people. I was back on Earth acting like a tour guide and tomorrow would be soon enough for us to have to get back to that other reality. Maybe I'm not as big a fruitcake as I've been thinking.

Then again, Tom, think about it. You actually believe you're standing in the middle of your apartment in Virginia City talking to a beautiful woman from another galaxy. You are willing to believe that the two of you are going to help solve a problem that has been plaguing the universe for millions of years. That oversized woman in starched white, the one with the cattle prod, is just outside that door, Tom, and she's going to get you. Cor-ah has to be the most wonderful figment of my imagination that I've ever come up with, but this simply can't be reality, can't be truth.

"Ow!" Cor-ah had promised once before to do that and she just pinched my skinny little butt, and I mean pinched. "Ow! Damn, pretty girl, you really pinched." I was rubbing the pinch out when another hand interrupted and the pinch didn't hurt quite so much anymore.

"This is reality, Tom. Now, take me for a walk, and then put me on one of those things, those vehicles." I had to chuckle over that and took her hand.

"Come on my little Torrian babe, let's check out Virginia City. You'll see things you've never thought of, and I just hope you get the feeling that none of this is real. Then, dear girl, guess who's going to get pinched?" That was met by another one of her grand smiles and we headed out the door and down the stairs.

"Such an evil mind," she said.

Virginia City today is a tourist Mecca created by the discovery in 1859 of the largest silver lode in North America. As with so many tourist areas much of the history is ignored for the opportunity to sell t-shirts emblazoned with strange commentary, tons of fudge made "old fashioned" because the sign says so, and representations of cowboys and Indians in what once was a mining community. But I know that Cor-ah will be enthralled by all of it. The noise of slot machines that scream winner when paying back twenty-five cents, with honky-tonk music that should be played on player pianos but is coming from compact discs, and with people dressed fashionably out-of-date. She will love it. I do, and I know where all the mistakes are made. I know what the real history is and I'm sometimes ashamed by what I hear store clerks tell the visitors. I still get a thrill walking up and down the streets that were walked by the same men that were responsible for creating the state of Nevada. Cor-ah will love my little town.

C Street was bustling with wagons filled with silver bearing ore more than a century ago, and today is filled with SUVs filled with squalling children and fat tourists. Not much change, really. It all reduces itself to money in the pocket for those living here. Cor-ah had a death-grip on my hand as we stepped out on the ancient and creaking boardwalks of the Comstock. She caught me totally by surprise by saying, "I've never heard so much noise."

Amazing, but she's right. All the time I was on Torry there was virtually no noise. No machinery with horns, belching engines, slot machines, hucksters, and children racing here and there. "This is just a normal day on Earth. I relished the quiet of Torry but didn't realize I was doing that. I couldn't put into words those differences that I felt standing before your home just a day or two ago. You immediately have picked up on one of the big differences between the way we live." She now had one hand intertwined with one of mine, and her other hand had a serious hold of one of my arms.

"Are you frightened?" That thought bothered the hell out of me. I didn't bring her here to be frightened, I brought her here to love Earth as I do. "Cor-ah, please don't be frightened, there is nothing that will harm you. I promise. Nothing." Oh, my. What have I done? There are so many differences and I didn't prepare her for one I didn't even recognize.

She didn't ask, just reacted. We were standing just outside my C Street doorway one moment and inside the apartment the next. She was terrified, and her eyes were darting about, looking for something that she could defend herself with. "Tom, how can you live like this? This isn't like Torry at all and you said I would love it. We must get back to Torry as soon as possible." I took both her hands in mine and we settled down onto a sofa in my living room. Even inside my hands hers were shaking, her lips were quivering and she had turned very white.

"I should be shot, Cor-ah. Please don't hate me, it never entered my mind that the noise and bustle of Earth would frighten you. When you live here it is a daily experience that isn't even thought of. Let me take you someplace that is just the opposite, but I will need your help. I know that you will not go with me in one of our vehicles, that would be the worst thing I could do right now." I was thinking of Silver Peak and the area around the cave, the area of strong energy. and where Yannow would be close so we could get back to Torry in a hurry if it came to that.

The thought came as a streak of lightning when I remembered Silver Peak and my first visit from Riba. I was as frightened then as Cor-ah is now. I wanted to bolt, to run, to get away from whatever was happening. I brought her here without first thinking of my own experience. I need to be horse whipped for giving her such a fright.

"There is a desert area south of here, it's where I first met Riba, it's where Yannow maintains a gate through time and space, and it's very quiet, I promise. I can put the area in your mind and you can take us there. Would that make you feel better?"

Such a simple thing really, I knew they had almost no machinery, even that shuttle we used to get to Toland made no noise, it was just a broom closet and there was no noise on the farm property now that I think about it, and throughout the universe all these people live the same. Noise I take for granted would be frightening, and yet Riba has never once mentioned it to me. It must be that he is used to it now and this was a direct assault on her system, the vehicles, the roar of the saloons and casinos, the smells, all different, all loud and distracting. What have I done? I have destroyed a love that I so much wanted for the rest of my life. I have hurt the one person in the universe that I love, and I feel lower than that toad she doesn't know anything about.

The thought of a toad brought a little smile to her glum and serious face. "I've never felt fear before, Tom. I've been afraid as I am about the nether people, about what is going to happen to Tetta, but out there, I feared for my life. The noise, and all the people bumping into each other, and being slightly anxious to start with, I feared for my life. Don't make me do that again, Tom. Please, don't make me do that again."

So much alike and yet so different. Will my dreams actually come to pass? Will I be able to spend my life with this beautiful woman? Now, I'm afraid. I almost got married once, it was a long time ago, and I have never wanted to again. That was a terrible experience that took my heart and tortured it as a wrecking ball tortures concrete and brick walls. When I walked into what we had talked of as our bedroom and found her in the arms of my own cousin, I died. I couldn't think of such a thing as marriage, of a permanent relationship for years afterwards and now I've found Cor-ah and lost her because I am stupid. I am stupid. Stupid. I should never have brought her here. I should allow Rohn-Da, her father to stand me against a wall and shoot my skinny ass.

"No, Tom. You aren't stupid, you aren't wrong. We should have talked about this before we did it. I'm just as upset as you are. I wanted to see your home, I wanted to come to Earth and be with you.

"No, you haven't lost me. It will take a lot more than this for you to get rid of me, hot shot. Oh, the stories we will have for our children."

Whoa, there's a thought that hasn't come up before. We talked about protecting, about not allowing a pregnancy, and she's talking about our children. Time now is standing still. I'm thinking of Corinne, remembering how we discussed children, discussed building our home, our lives, our family, and how badly it ended. Time, it keeps popping its head into my life at the strangest time, and without any warning. I'm in a conversation with a dream, discussing children, our children, our lives, our home. Amazing. Time, yes and, of course, the never-ending question of the family of man. How much of this am I going to be able to remember? This has to be written down, has to be known. Children. Children?

"Cor-ah, I love you very much, I want to be with you forever, whatever the hell that means anymore. How can there be a forever if reality is based on where we are at the time?   Cor-ah, my mind is helpless right now.   Our children?"

"But, you will never ever get me into one of those things."   She jerked her head toward the window and I knew instantly she meant vehicle.   My pretty little yellow Jeep pickup will just have to rust away because I will spend the rest of my life on Torry except for visits to Earth either by myself or with Riba.

"Do you remember when papa gave you that little drink and you said it was like beer on Earth?   Do you remember?   Well, I want a taste without leaving this room." I could almost picture her stamping her little foot. 'Without leaving this room.'   It had that good sound to it, like she wasn't frightened to death anymore but she wasn't willing to search for the dragon either.

I went over to the refrigerator and got out a couple of bottles of Sam Adams Pale Ale.   "Here darling lady. This is what I was telling Rohn-Da about."   She took a long draught and looked straight into my eyes, a grand and glorious smile spreading across her face.   That's better, I thought.   That's better.   I actually did something right for the first time today.

"Papa will like this."   She took another deep drink and looked at me.   "You are the nicest man I've ever met and I want to spend the rest of my life with you.   I told my family that, even though you couldn't hear me, and now I'm telling you.   I was very much terrified by walking out on that scene outside earlier, but now I know that it is the essence of how you live.   If I'm going to be your woman and you are going to be my man then we have to be able to understand each other.   You came to Torry, Tom, probably not on your own volition if I know Riba, but you came, and you fell in love with how we live, with how we think, and with me.

"Now I'm on Earth and I have embarrassed you. I'm sorry. I want to learn about Earth, about humans, mostly, I want to know everything about you."

"You have not embarrassed me in any way Cor-ah. I took advantage of you by bringing you here without first telling you about how we live. I'm embarrassed by the way I treated you. I'm sorry from deep in my soul. Please forgive me and let me introduce you to Earth properly." She reached out and took my hand and walked me into the bedroom. Ah, the pleasures of the family of man.

All thoughts of Virginia City, vehicles, clamoring slot machines, nether people, Quarians, all thoughts that don't include the word, Cor-ah are forbidden for the next several hours. It's time for us, on Earth, in my apartment, in our bed.

The bedroom of my apartment has large windows facing east and sunrise flooded the room, and was inconsequential compared to Cor-ah's smile.

"Hi, hot shot. I like the way humans make those from other galaxies feel right at home." It was just a few hours ago that I was afraid I had lost this galactic charger, and now she is telling me she and I will be one forever. Differences and all. And with children.

"I'll bet I can walk down that street without one single panic attack today. You have to feed me first, but I bet I can." We're going to destroy a couple of huge omelets first, and then we're going to take a little walk early enough that the boardwalks of Virginia City won't be crowded.

"Ever had huevos rancheros? No? That will be down the line. Today, a mushroom omelet with three delightful cheeses. Don't you wrinkle your nose at me, young lady. I still have access to toads you know.

"We'll even have a beer in the Bucket of Blood, my Torrian beauty." The look on her face wasn't fear, but one hell of a question danced across her mug. "The Bucket of

Blood is the oldest saloon in Virginia City and we will have a drink there." There really was relief in her face. I love this little intergalactic beauty. We spent a few more minutes, several actually, watching the sun make its way up into the sky and finally got moving. She stood over me like a mother hen as I made breakfast, watched me clean and cook the mushrooms and onions, watched as I broke the eggs and mixed them up, watched as I poured the omelets in the buttered pan and put the mushrooms, onions, and some of the cheese over the eggs.

She was so close I had to move her back a couple of times, and she almost burned herself on the pan when I turned the eggs out onto the plates. "There, pretty girl, there is your first mushroom omelet. Done the human way."

"Okay, big guy, you do the cooking in our family."

We walked for hours up and down the steep hills of Virginia City, visited tourist traps, some really good, had a cold beer at the Bucket of Blood and made it back to the apartment late in the afternoon. "You don't really like fudge, do you?" She had eaten at least half a pound of the rich chocolate candy while I had one little taste.

"I'm going to try to make some of this stuff with Torry ingredients. I love fudge, Tom." We knew our time on Earth was running out. It was time to get back to work.

"If I show you on a map where we need to go to meet Yannow, will you be able to take us there?" It was the only area of energy that I knew about and it was 250 miles from where we were.

"Just think in your mind where we need to be, Tom and we'll be there. When you and Riba went there was there any special time involved?"

"The first time was in the present, but we didn't see Yannow. The only time I've seen Yannow was at a time 8,000 years before my birth."

I looked at her, she smiled, and we were sitting in the sand in a cave 8,000 years before my birth, making marks in the sand with our fingers. The smile never changed. How the hell do they do that? One minute sitting on a couch in my living room, next minute sitting in the sand, not just 250 miles south but 8,000 years before. Impossible. Jesus, did I turn the coffeepot off?

"Hello, Yannow. I'm Cor-ah and this is..."

"Yes, human Tom. You are getting around aren't you? It's nice to see you. You wish to return to Torry?"

"Yes, Yannow. We've had a nice visit, Cor-ah has never been on Earth before and I wanted her to know about my planet. We need to get back to work, now. Have you heard anything from Riba in the last day or two?"

"No, but I know there have been meetings going on. You wish to go to Torry not to the Universal Council?"

"Well, yes, please. I wonder, Yannow, would it be possible to take a few minutes and look around outside the cave? I've been here so many times, always during my time, that I would like to see it in this time. And let Cor-ah see Earth in a different light from that of Virginia City." This would be my first opportunity to see these hillsides as they were at the time I believe the petroglyphs were etched into the stone. My heart was beating as fast as I could remember it and I was also filled with that tinge of trepidation that comes from possibly looking into the unknown. What will I do if we meet one of the people from this time? They will be as afraid of us as we will be of them. Thousands of questions are crowding my mind and Yannow doesn't wait for an opportunity to speak, just jumps in.

"That would be fine, Tom. Just come back here and mark your spot in the sign. I'll be here when you need me." I looked at Cor-ah and was met with a seriously questioning look.

"It's okay. There isn't anything to fear. I've told you about my work on Earth, and the time we're in right now is when the etchings on the rocks were made. I think. We can take a little walk outside this cave and you can see where I was exploring the day I met Riba." I took a look outside the cave and pointed to a hillside about two hundred feet away. "That's where I was standing when Riba appeared the first time."

We got soaked of course because of the waterfall just outside the cave, but this time it was almost a fun venture. Riba was not there to shake his head at me. I was amazed at the changes in the Silver Peak Playa from how it looks in my time. The playa is a desert during my time but right now we were looking at a sea, a large and open sea, huge in magnitude. The mountains that would have been where the mining community of Tonopah would be eight thousand years from now were islands, not very big islands I might add, and Lone Mountain, home to huge desert big horn sheep in today's time looms almost as a threat, big and black and fierce looking as it stands as a silent island sentry. There was a tremendous amount of flora. In my time, there was just scrub brush, a few spindly piñon pines, a cedar or two and that's it.

Large trees were in profusion, the rocks were not covered in lichen, nor did they have any markings on them. One set of rocks that I knew had petroglyphs written on them was blank. Cor-ah was mesmerized by the beauty.

"This is so much different from Virginia City. So calm and beautiful. Show me these rock etchings you like to study." I couldn't. They weren't there. I was deeply disappointed, and we walked back to the cave. There were no indigenous people standing around, there were no rock writings, there was nothing to indicate that people lived in the area of the cave.

"We're too early, Cor-ah." That wasn't all bad. I mean, if eight thousand years was too early, would six thousand be right? "It just means we'll have to come back another time. The one thing I know for a fact is, they did live in this area, and if we can pin the time down, we will be writing the history books." There it was again, writing, books, a look of confusion on her face. "We have a lot to discuss, my friend. A lot." I wonder why I hadn't shown any of my books to Cor-ah when we were in my apartment? Why didn't that occur to me? "When we are here next time, I'll introduce you to books, little lady. And, I guess I'll have to teach you to read as well." All I got back was a look of complete lack of understanding. Man, is my work cut out or what?

We walked into the cave, called for Yannow so he could send us back to Torry in Cor-ah's time. She had my hand, squeezed it a bit, and smiled at me. "You were right, Tom. We are very much alike and very much different. I like Earth, but it will take me a long time to get used to all that noise. Maybe we'll make our home here, 8,000 years before your birth." She nodded and I knew what was about to happen. A first.

Chapter Nine

Cor-ah shot me a smile and a wink, and I said a quiet thank you for the heads up. I don't know if the word love is acceptable in our relationship just yet, but it certainly can't be far away. Of course, it's love. Don't be stupid again, Tom. It's love. Here's a woman who knows who she is, is proud of that, and is a born leader, all features in a woman I've come to appreciate. I'm letting my mind take a little jaunt here, and I know everyone is picking up on my thoughts, but it's one of those times I simply can't let it rest, as Riba usually instructs.

We were standing in front of her home on Torry watching a glorious sunrise. Strawberry clouds melded into orange smoothies, and a cobalt sky warmed to a more sensuous aqua. I've learned, I think that it really is all the same God that makes this thing we call a universe work. "We have as many sunrises as we want, eh girl? One on Earth just a few hours ago and now another on Torry." There was just a smudge of fudge on the corner of her mouth and when she caught me looking, quickly wiped it away. Luckily, Tanda showed up just then and saved me from getting a tongue-lashing. "There's your mom."

"I'm glad you're back. Riba and Rohn-Da want you at Council, Tom. It might be a good idea if you go, too, Cor-ah. I'm so worried about Tetta. Can something be done, anything? I love my little girl, Tom, I could never allow all of that to just go away. It can't be done. Please." She was as frightened right now as Cor-ah was on Earth, and she and Cor-ah were holding on to each other, crying, sobbing actually, pleading with me. Torry women are the dominant sex, but like mama bears everywhere, they are still mothers and their babies come first.

My God, I'm just a writer, a guy who loves the old people. How did all this come about and am I in any kind

of position to change anything? Damn those nether people.
"We'll go to Council, and we'll come up with an answer,
Tanda.   An answer that will not include losing Tetta.   I
don't know how, but we will." Cor-ah put her arms around
me, smiled at her mother and said about the same thing.

"Mama, little Tetta will be fine.   I've just been to
Earth with Tom, and I have a better understanding of why
he is the way he is. I trust him completely and I know that
he only has our best interests in his heart. It will be okay,
mama," and we were sitting at council. My sense of humor
makes me want to Whoosh every time this happens, but
right now, I'm not in any kind of humorous mood.   The
thought of lives being lost is more than I can accept.   It
won't happen. Now, my God, I've got a woman who says
we can have children. We can be together forever.

"Did you see the look on Tanda's face when you
said you had come to Earth with me? And we left before
she could fully understand. What will she say when we tell
her about our children?"   What a great life it would be,
having this Torrian woman at my side, traveling through
the universe, maybe even as an ambassador at large or
some such, continuing at the same time, my delving into so
many different histories.   When we're alone again,
whenever that might be, I have to remember to talk to her
about this, and particularly the histories.

I would have immediate access to actual facts in
history, being able to be on the spot, so to speak. If I was
writing about the tableaus we find on rocks, I would be able
to step back in time and discover their true meaning, I
would know the people who etched the 'glyphs, and
understand why they did it. I wouldn't have to limit these
historical records to just the Earth, but could include so
many societies that I've just begun to meet.

I have discovered several things that are common
on Earth and are known in other galaxies as well. Beer, for
instance, is not just an Earth thing, but is well known in

many parts of the universe. I wonder if that is the case with rock writing? I wonder if when the Torrians first began to emerge as a people following the visit by Sonneth that they also made their mark so to speak on rocks? I might be able to tie the histories of the universe together into one large package and teach this concept of the universal man after all.

I think I may have found the true meaning of my life, to move about all the various planes of reality, teach this to humans, and teach others about the universe as a whole, not complicated by regional difficulties such as the Earth experiences today. The human mind is so fast at learning, and that ability will be compounded exponentially because of my adventures with the Universal Council. I can picture myself lecturing to history majors, even taking the class to a point in history that's under discussion.

Imagine a conversation with Shakespeare, an evening with Mozart, a week, nay a lifetime, with Socrates. Our knowledge of ourselves would be as complete as possible. The only challenge would be ethical, not to change history while learning its truths. We don't know a lot about these nether people, but what we do know is frightening as it relates to the universe, but what about how it relates to the history of humankind? Socrates sticks in my mind for a moment and I'm again thinking that the human race not only produced such a man as Socrates but also one as hateful as Hitler. Is that the work of the Nether Gene as I'm beginning to think of it?

Can we take what we know about how their genes are affecting us and use that to our benefit? If we know, for instance, that we are selfish, cruel, unkind in so many instances, can it be possible to genetically alter those attributes right out of future generations?

It's surely something for me to discuss with my hosts. Genetically accepting what has happened, and altering it for future generations may be an answer for the rest of the universe as well. Forcing the nether people to return to their own universe may be a larger problem than simply correcting the current situation. If we can move through time and space, we can stop future infestations, and by genetically altering what has already happened, we won't have to change history. The generations on Torry, for instance, won't be lost, and future generations will be as Torrian as those not affected in the first place.

This is as close as I can get to solving this problem without having to alter history, the worst possible thing we could do. I wonder how, since I'm just a human, I can get these ideas before Qadroth and the Council?

"You already have, human Tom." Qadroth was smiling broadly as he said this, and others in the chamber were looking at me with an intensity I hadn't seen before. "Even though we've been discussing the problem for several days, your proposals are more in line with how we would like to end the problem of the nether people. Not one of your ideas was brought up by a member of the Council. I'm more and more amazed at the way the human mind works. Actually, Tom, I'm impressed with the logic of your mind, uncontrolled as it is." Why do I have the feeling that there is more to this than his words?

Qadroth knows more than what he is letting on, understands more about what all these discussions have been about, and is holding back. He seems to understand this conceptual thinking idea that Rohn-Da says he has never understood. Cor-ah knows most of what I talk about but not until it is brought up. Her mind is so quick. Qadroth is looking at me, almost with some kind of clandestine gleam in those bright eyes. He does know something that hasn't been brought up before. He continues his thoughts to the rest of the council.

"If we know which Torrians have had relationships with a nether person, we will know how to alter the genetic code of any offspring that may occur. The following generation will again be Torrian. Your mind is splendid the way it works through problems like this. It will take a massive amount of research, however, to break that genetic code and discover just what will have to be eliminated. Just what exactly is the nether genetic code that creates so much chaos in various subspecies?"

He just said, "a massive amount of research," but for all this time I've been led to believe that these people don't understand the concept of research, of histories, of knowledge about happenings in earlier times. This Quarian is holding a lot back, knows much more than anyone else in this room. That is how the Quarians keep their hold on the Universal Council, I'll bet, not letting on to certain facts and ideas. That is why Riba has always frightened me to a degree and Rohn-Da has never frightened me.

This is the control factor. Is this why there are no books, no education facilities, no art? By never introducing such things eons ago, and only letting "the children" understand what Quarians let be available, there is complete control. The main question that I must answer is, why? Why the complete control at all costs?

Even though I know I don't have to voice my ideas, sometimes I feel I must hear my own thoughts as I speak to these people. "What if some of the nether people were female? We don't know for sure that only males came through those universal portals, and how did they know what to say or how to use the signs to get through the gates in the first place?

"Is there a channel, a conduit between the universes, and if there is, why do the nether people know about it, and you on the Council apparently don't? If there is such a thing, why hasn't it been sealed off in some way? I know I'm ahead of the discussion, but the concept of universal travel hasn't really been fully taught to me.

"Let's say we can stop the nether people in the Torrian infestation, what's to stop them from simply moving on to another galaxy?" If intent looks could maim or kill, I'd be one dead sucker right now. Every member of the Council is staring at me, some shaking their heads.

"This is amazing." Qadroth stands up, glances at just about every person in attendance. "Here we are discussing how not to end the lives of a small number of people on Torry, and Tom is the only member of the Council who has actually recognized the real problem. It isn't that they have come, but how did they come, and how do we stop future invasions? We are fully aware the Marq system was invaded probably millions of years ago, and it will be impossible to change that without altering the entire history of that galaxy, in particular the history of those from the planet Earth, however genetic alteration may be possible.

"Okay, we are fully aware that Torry has been invaded recently and we can't take a chance on altering that history either, but as Tom has said, genetically we can probably cure the problem without jeopardizing any lives. But, as Tom again has pointed out, we have not solved the major problem." He had been marching around the outside of the gathered group, his long silver hair actually blowing around in his self-made breeze, talking in loud clear tones, for my benefit, I'm sure since I can't do their mind gymnastics. He went back to his seat at the head of the table. He is this grand leader of the universe, his brow wrinkled but every strand of hair in place, eyes shining, smiling benignly on his subjects, yes, one could read at a glance that he is the leader. He settled in, took in the table at a glance, and continued.

"We need to get together with all the gate keepers to see if there is a flaw in our way of doing things that has let the nether people in. That is the most important thing we can do at this moment.

"Tene, you head up this commission and pick whomever you want to work with you. Find out how these

135

nether people are able to simply show up, how they know how to get here, and yet we don't have any idea how to get there. I'm the one hundred and thirty second chairman of this Council, and in the last several million years, I've not heard of a way for us to enter another universe. It is just recently I've even been aware of a second universe. Obviously, the nether people have known of our universe for some time."

That was really hard for me to accept. These people have been able to travel through time, space, speak and move about with just their minds, and most of what we're discussing is all but brand new to them. Somebody somewhere isn't telling the truth, is holding back some kind of information, and the real answer to this enigma is who is holding back and why. Cor-ah could feel my questions, could understand it all, and gave me a gentle tap, similar to what I had done on Toland. She was saying, 'shut up, Tom. Shut up now'.

All about the table, heads are turning, and it appears that conversations are being held, internally. By looking at each other, they are able to converse, and others around them are also able to understand, and I'm not picking up a shred of what's being debated or discussed.

"Qadroth, on many occasions, you've mentioned Clotero in such a manner that I believe him to be the god of the universe, the one responsible for bringing order out of chaos, probably creating two universal entities, one opposite the other, that concept of likes and opposites, for balance. Would it be possible then, that if Clotero is the god of this universe there would be a god of the other? Is what we are facing actually a contest between the two gods, in which the concept of chaos is not unattractive to the god of the nether universe?" This seemed to open a great debate, with everyone in the room taking part.

Cor-ah took my hand in hers, and was holding on tightly, but I could tell that she was also taking part in the debate.   Qadroth spoke first among the council members. "Go home to your galaxies, to your families, and consider all that we have heard today.   We will meet again in two days, and hopefully we will have some answers.

"Tom, what you have brought to this council table is amazing.   We have never had a human sit with us as you're doing and the way your mind is able to conceptualize what may be happening is something that hasn't happened before.   There is much to learn from our human cousins, even if the population of the planet isn't quite ready to join the Council.   Tom, because of what you have done, I am now ready to say, we should have at least one representative from the Marq system on our Universal Council from this day forward."

One minute I was at Council, holding hands with Cor-ah, and the next, I was back at my own kitchen table in Virginia City, Nevada, Earth, Marq System, pondering the questioning eyes of dear old Riba.   I had to glance over though, just to make sure the coffeepot was off. "Questions, Tom.   I have questions."   Riba has never put a question to me.   "Where should we start?   This is the most complex problem I've ever had to discuss with anyone, more or less with a human mind, so jumbled, so able to see through problems."   He managed the little jibe right in the middle of praise.   The old Aztec is holding his own.

"Riba, tell me what you think about this invasion. Is it a case of the nether people actually wanting chaos? It's logical from my thinking, but how do you look at the situation?

"Here on Earth, in the current teaching of gods and whatnot, there is always a good and an evil.   A universal god rules over heaven and Earth, while an evil god, usually referred to as the devil, rules over hell.   The common belief is that the two gods fought at one time, and this is how they divided the realm.   From what we have seen with the nether people, that second universe could very well be what

137

earthlings refer to as hell, an evil place in which evil people reign."

"Simplistic, Tom, even naive, but it also describes in very basic terms what we are seeing." Riba became contemplative, usually meaning he was compartmentalizing that broad mind of his. "My understanding of the universe is such that I recognize how the various subspecies came to be, and how over millions of your years they have evolved into what you have seen. I'm also aware that at some point after the human subspecies was created, the nether people came and altered the evolutionary process we had started.

"What I'm having a most difficult time understanding, is how the nether people came to be in our universe in the first place. Until you brought that up, the question had never occurred to me. It was simply a case of they are here, what do we do about it? Now the question becomes, how did they get here, and how do we, one; force them back into their own universe, and two; prohibit a return?

"Tom, I don't have the slightest idea how to enter their universe. How is it they know how to enter ours? The ideas of two entities, our Clotero, omnipotent in every sense, but having an equal in another universe is hard to comprehend. It would tarnish the concept of omnipotence, wouldn't it?" The old guy was pacing around my kitchen, hands clasping behind his back, head shaking as thoughts rambled about, with the strangeness of a human mind, and not coming up with answers. A position the star traveler hasn't been in before.

"I think we need to talk with Yannow."

"Yes, old one. He specifically told us he had let them in because they knew all the proper signs and devices. Somehow, these people knew how to get through his gate." Riba kept right on pacing, almost as if he hadn't heard what I was saying. "Are you holding a conversation with someone else?"

"No.   But I think I have reached at least part of an answer.   I want you and Cor-ah to go back to Toland, Tom, and make friends with that nether person.   Pick his brain, to use one of your delightful metaphors, and learn everything you can.

"It was you who said they work on opposite principals as we, so getting him to spill his guts shouldn't be too difficult."   He loved using Earth aphorisms because they were so much not like him.   Spill his guts, indeed, old one.

Kantor El will want to brag up a storm, though, and of course, the thought of spending more time with delicious Cor-ah was splendid.   I've only been away from her for...what?   I don't know.   It seems like we were sitting together just moments ago, although I also feel we've been apart for a long time.   Time, it keeps creeping into my thoughts, and yet, we've proved, time is relative to, again, what?   I have no idea where I should look into an Earth sky to find Torry, how can I imagine what kind of time separation there might be between where I am and where she is?   And it wasn't that many years ago that Einstein told us about bending time as it moves through the universe. And light, too. Einstein should be here, not me.

I know I want to be where she is, and together at the same time.   Cor-ah and I have been called on to do good works, something the nether people can't understand. "Yes, Riba, my old friend, Cor-ah and I will allow this Kantor El to do the opposite, and be proud of it, and we will learn something.

"And you, old one, what will you be doing?"   I didn't mean to say that out loud, calling Riba old one out loud, damn me, that's twice now.

"You've always called me, 'old one,' Tom.   Don't be embarrassed by saying it out loud.   When we were at Council, you were wondering how we are able to converse with our minds.   It's more complicated than forcing thoughts to move between our minds.

"Remember me telling you about compartmentalizing our thinking?   Our brain functions? That is one of the reasons we are hard pressed sometimes understanding you because you don't have any regimen what so ever to your thinking.   Your mind is in what we would call chaos, spinning out of control, yet making strong and obvious conclusions.   Your mind is exploding with thought at all times and not necessarily related to a current conversation.

"We can turn off certain functions of the mind in order to concentrate on one item at a time.   This gives extreme power to the one thought process we are working on and our minds actually accept other's thoughts while transmitting our own.   I think when our brains developed this power, your brain was developing these other powers, your ability to conceptualize, for instance.   You are able to break a problem down into its basic form and work from there.   I can't do that.

"Sometimes, Tom, I think you see an answer before you see a question.   Is that a part of the abstract process, the human ability to work through problems after breaking them into smaller pieces?"   Riba just hit on one of the ways that problems are solved.   We sometimes know something but don't know why, and thus we want to find out why. Quarians don't do that.   Riba answered his own thought.

"We see the problem, but don't take it apart.   We compartmentalize our thinking process where you seem to compartmentalize what's being thought or discussed.   It will be interesting to discover if this is from nether world genes, or whether it's simply a human evolvement. Problem solving has never been something we have concentrated on simply because from our point of view, most of the problems we face have been faced before, and thus, have already been solved."

Riba just spelled out the Quarian ego. All the problems have been solved so we don't need to ask questions. They don't ask questions, they know nothing of their history, and there seems to be no educational system in any of the galaxies because of this Quarian mind-set. How will one be able to teach those that believe they know everything already? Riba looked at me, almost with disdain as he continued.

"You see problems we just pass over. How did the nether people know how to get here? Why don't we know how to get there? Why go to Torry instead of staying on Earth? That's what makes you so much different from us and what makes you so valuable to this mystery."

Riba's pacing had slowed perceptively as he moved deeper into his thoughts. I've never heard him talk this way before, and I have learned as much about him and Quarians in general these last few moments, as he has apparently learned about us, and the old Aztec wasn't through.

"While you're on Torry, I'm going to visit with Yannow and other gate keepers. I want us to meet with the Council in a day or two, so try to gain as much information as you can from your nether friend. Hopefully, between all of us, including that group Tene is leading, we'll be able to prepare a defense against this invasion, and what to do about those who are nether progeny." He had a grip on the back of a chair as he spoke, and I could feel his frustration.

This is a wonderful moment in our relationship. Riba is talking with me as an equal, and I'm accepting him for the individual he is instead of the old taskmaster, bender of time and space. Riba is a deep person, unlike, for instance, Tene who is only surface and can't seem to think in the manner that I do and as, apparently Riba does and this is the first time that the old Aztec and I have had a serious one-on-one conversation, discussion, if you will. In the future, I want to be able to sit at this table in my apartment with Riba, Rohn-Da, and Cor-ah and have just enough beer to let the philosopher in each of us come to the surface. What an evening that will be. We might even get Qadroth to come to the party along with Socrates for some real intellectual discussion.

"Before I go, old friend, I have a big question for you. I brought Cor-ah to Earth for a couple of days and she was terrified of the noise and hubbub around her. I figured it out, but I've never seen you upset about anything you've found here. She was ready to go back to Torry within seconds of stepping outside this apartment, yet you go about as if you've lived here your whole life."

"Cor-ah hasn't traveled as I have, Tom. The incessant noise is more than bothersome to me, but I've gotten used to it. You will find that Rohn-Da will not be disturbed by the racket and turmoil. He has traveled extensively as I have and isn't disturbed by other cultures. This was one of the few times Cor-ah has been away from Torry and the safety of her family."

Interestingly, I could also feel my impending move through space and time. I may be learning something after all.

Chapter Ten

Although I didn't know where I would end up, I knew this time I was going somewhere. Did Riba give me a mind signal, or was I just a bit perceptive? Either way, I'm sitting under a rock overhang in the Nevada desert just outside Silver Peak, apparently in my own time as I'm beginning to think of it. It took just moments, getting the proper signs marked in the sand, and Yannow was standing beside me. I've been to places I've never heard of, seen things almost impossible to describe, and yet, and remember this is the third or fourth time I've met Yannow, I'm still incredulous. I'm having a conversation with Yeti.

As far as I can understand, I'm probably the only human being not associated with being a shaman, alive today that can say that. One would think there would be some serious anxiety associated with standing next to a creature that stands well over seven feet tall and is covered in thick fur, but because of his demeanor, I'm completely at ease. There's a gentleness about Yannow and even a reverence, if that word can be used in this context. I can picture Yannow giving a lecture, almost preaching if you will, and obviously would have everyone's attention from the first.

Where was he before I used the signs and called him to me? Is his dimension yet another place, another time? Riba will come when I call for him, also, and now Yannow comes when the proper sign is marked in the sand. But from where? In times past, humans have unexpectedly come upon Yeti, and yet I can't believe this goliath simply lives somewhere near this cave and just waits for someone to call. I must have a million questions and very few answers.

The legends of the great southwest are true, the experiences of the Himalayan trekkers is proven, the stories coming from the California and Oregon forests are real. I'm having a conversation with Yannow, the keeper of the gate. What a formidable experience if one should accidentally come upon him, and it's understandable the stories relating to such experiences are so wild that they are all but unbelievable.   In all my future adventures, on my own Earth, or where ever my travels take me, nothing will compare in my mind to meeting Yannow.

That brings up a thought that I've had several times during these trips and visits.   Who the hell will believe anything I say if I try to relate any of this?   "Yeti, Tom?" "Been in the sun again, old man?"   "Visiting planets where, Tom?" Always accompanied by gales of laughter, pokes in the ribs, ending all thoughts of continuing a conversation. Speaking of which, my friend Yannow is here talking to me.   The idea of bringing an editor along for a visit one day really catches me by surprise and I can see the surprise on Yannow's face as well.   He's thinking, 'editor?'

"I see Riba has taught you right, human Tom.   You have been busy these last few days haven't you?"   The voice is hollow as before but there are hints of a smile, a crinkling of the eyes as he says this.   Yannow has a sense of humor.   "It will take just another moment, and you'll be at Rohn-Da's home on Torry.   I understand Riba is also planning to come here.   Good, I'm looking forward to discussing this nether world problem.   Most perplexing, human Tom.   Have a good journey."

Yannow was expecting me and knew that Riba was also planning a journey soon.   Yannow has powers and abilities far beyond anything I can comprehend, as does Riba, Rohn-Da, even Cor-ah, but he seems to know things in advance and I haven't noticed that in the others.   Many are the tales told around Native American campfires dealing with the gateways to other planes of existence, to other places and always there are gatekeepers.   What would it take to spend two or three days with this wonderful creature called Yannow?

Tanda was smiling a welcome as I found myself on that gravel pathway to her home. A light breeze brought all the flavor of the colorful plants and flowers, cream puff clouds danced across the Torrian sky, and I had the distinct feeling that I had come home.

"You knew I was coming?"

"Riba sent word you would be coming. Cor-ah will be here shortly. Rohn-Da is looking forward to seeing you again." She had a worried look about her, and it didn't take a genius to know why. After all, she could lose a daughter in this mess. "Have you discovered some way of correcting what's happened? Are some of us here going to lose loved ones?" Tanda was trying to hold back the tears, but they were coming anyway. She wrapped her arms around herself, hugged herself as tightly as anyone could, and moaned, "My baby. I love Tetta even if she is part nether." This is mama bear, willing to take on the universe to save her cub.

It was I that first put the thought of changing history into play and I've never felt lower at this moment. At least I might have some good news for Tanda and other families on Torry. The thought of simply doing away with children of these affairs is murder, ethnic cleansing, another horrible holocaust, and it was a human that came up with the idea. Thankfully, that idea never got past being just discussed and rejected.

We walked toward the house, I had my arm around Tanda's shoulder and she was holding my hand in a grip of immense strength. One doesn't get a chance to pick one's family often in this life and right now I'm the luckiest man in the world, actually in the universe and for all time. Time and space mean nothing to this traveler, I smugly told myself.

Torrian women may be the dominant sex, but as everywhere, they are nurturing and protecting mothers and so much like humans. I do love this family. This is my family now, one that I will protect and love. "At Council we discussed many things, and I think we can correct most of the problems without having to alter history. There are still things to work out, Tanda, but Tetta and other children like her on Torry are going to be safe." I was telling her about the possible manipulation of nether genes as we walked to the house.

The impact of all of this is also taking a toll on my mental state. I no longer believe I'm mad, while I'm also confused about everything that's happening. I'm on a planet in a galaxy that just a short time ago I'd never heard of. I've accepted an appointment to a Universal Council, and I'm standing in the living room of a couple whose eldest daughter I think I'm in love with. At the same time, I'm talking about saving the life of another daughter who came into being because mama couldn't keep her panties on, and it doesn't bother either daddy or the kids.

We all have our own personal morals, ethics, and societal values, and I'm completely in agreement with the mores of Torry, even if they are dramatically different from those of Earth. Something, though, still bothers the hell out of me. Doesn't anyone have a profession, a job? Also, no one ever discusses a history of any kind. It's hard to look around this beautiful home and not see any books, not anything that might serve as a means of learning. There are no newspapers or magazines, there doesn't seem to be any entertainment appliances either. No television or radio, I haven't heard anyone discuss having a game of some kind. This universal family of man is devoid of much of what I would consider essential. It's the pleasure element and the intellectual element that seems to be missing from these lives. I'm reminded how seriously the Quarians take all aspects of life and I'm developing a picture of a possible

Quarian effort to keep pleasure out of the lives of the subspecies. That is not a good thought, but it stays in my mind, even as Tanda and I talk.

What pleasure I've seen comes from simple things like eating well, traveling to vacation spots, being with each other. If there aren't any cities as I would recognize, where do they shop? If no one seems to have a job, where does the means to have a home, clothes, and food come from? If I'm not crazy, I'll drive myself there soon with all these questions.

Inside, Rohn-Da was waiting for us, and he apparently had already picked up on what had happened at Council. "I'm glad Tetta is going to be alright. Tanda and I were very worried about all the children that might have come to us because of the nether people." He settled into a chair and nodded as if he was saying, 'yes, all is okay'. It isn't all okay, we both know that, but it is better than it was.

Another thought was working its way through the fog I call a brain and that dealt with science. If we're going to separate these genes, those from this universe and those from the nether, are there people in any of the galaxies that are capable of the work? Which brings me right back to history, jobs, and education

"Rohn-Da, Tanda, on Earth I'm a writer, a reporter of history, that's how I make my living, how I earn my bread and water, dealing with ancient people and their societies. Earth, like most of the universe, has been around for a long time, and her people have histories that go back into the millions of years. How is the history of Torry, or for that matter, the universe taught? I haven't seen any books in your home, and I haven't heard anyone discuss what happened here in the past.

"I spend hundreds of hours learning the complexities of history, politics, religion, morals of some of the societies on Earth. Learning from your point however, must be so much more complex, knowing other subspecies, for instance, other galaxies. I have trouble with Earth history. You must have massive libraries set aside just for history. How is history taught on Torry, or in the universe?"

Such an easy question, and yet, all I'm getting back for an answer are blank stares, even between themselves. I tried again, combining history and education.

"History is taught as soon as a child is old enough to read, and there are literally thousands of people on Earth that make their living teaching and researching history. You're giving me the impression you don't have any idea what I'm talking about."

Rohn-Da and Tanda didn't know what I was talking about. It appears that history is not something that's known, discussed, taught, or even understood. Imagine a universe filled with subspecies from thousands of galaxies, and the only people interested in history live on the only planet not allowed in their Universal Council. I may have found my calling as a teacher if I should be lucky enough to spend the rest of my life here.

"Maybe I didn't phrase my question properly. Why do you build your houses in cylindrical form?" Rohn-Da was looking at me in complete wonder, and Tanda, wanting to give some sort of response, just shrugged. "All right, then, I heard Qadroth mention he was the one hundred and something leader of the Universal Council. How will the next leader be determined? Who was the leader before Qadroth?" I don't think the questions had ever been asked before because all I got was that continuing blank stare from both.

"It seems there may be more to our differences than just the ability to speak with your minds. You don't teach or learn any kind of history about your people, your planet, your galaxy? How do you educate the young people?" Still, the two aren't saying a word, and I'm either amazed or shocked, I don't know which. I'm involved with a society that has no education system.

This is impossible to understand and, remembering the conversations at Council, it isn't just this society but the entire universe. Cor-ah and I have had some conversations in which she could not understand certain things I was talking about. On the other hand, as soon as I explained them, she fully understood. Torrians are capable of learning, I'm sure the Quarians are as well, yet no one is taught.

How do they learn about who they are if there are no books and no schools, no libraries? We feel that learning about who we are, what makes us tick, is extremely important, we write thousands of volumes on why our forefathers did this and that, and these people don't know who their forefathers even are.

"I think I understand what you're asking, Tom, but I don't have an answer because there is no answer." Tanda was confused, but continued. "We are born with certain knowledge and it isn't necessary to try to understand more than that. The Quarian leaders have always seen to it that we know what we need to know." That's what Riba says, that's what Qadroth was getting at when he said the council never entertained the question of how to stop further nether invasions. This is why nobody asks questions. They believe they already know everything worth knowing because the Quarians told them so.

Qadroth said no one had ever given my questions any thought before. How do the nether people know how to get here? A question as simple as this and it has never been thought of? The entire Torrian galaxy has no use for history? Don't they even understand the concept of understanding the past? The nether people are having a field day, actually field millions of years, and the question of how they knew how to get here has never been asked. Once again, Tom, amazing.

I'm beginning to understand how things work in this universe. Minds so advanced in one direction, that is focusing, communicating, traveling through space and time mentally, that the concept of learning something new, asking questions about why something happens, or how to correct something, never enters their minds. They have lost the concept of wanting to know, to learn from the past, to project that learning to the future. They do not learn. What a revelation. These mind boggling abilities I've been envying have actually acted as barriers to their ability to think. A concept cannot be rolled around the head bone and conjured into something concrete. They think I have superior abilities at being able to understand certain concepts, even those abstract at times, when in reality, they have forced that ability from their own minds.

The idea of people from an opposite universe coming to this universe, copulating with anyone available in order to create what we know as chaos is just something that happened. It isn't necessary to ask why or how. Simply knowing they are here is the complete answer. "As we just said, Rohn-Da and Tanda, there are some distinct differences between us. Everything we've just discussed can be overcome so easily, but it's amazing that none of these concepts have ever been discussed on Torry or anywhere else in the universe. Amazing." I found after that little speech that I had stood up and was almost giving a lecture. Calm down, Tom, or in the words of Riba, let it rest.

Cor-ah has said more than once that she doesn't understand how my mind works, and I'm sitting here thinking to myself that I don't have a clue how Torry minds work. Knowing you know everything worth knowing is pretty damned arrogant in my mind, but I remember Riba and Qadroth both saying the Quarians are pretty arrogant. How does one grow to adulthood without asking one's self questions? Who am I? Why am I here? Since we all started with Quarian genes it was the human that evolved differently.

History wouldn't mean anything if one couldn't use that history as a learning tool for something in the future. There would not be a need to educate a child if the thinking processes needed for conceptualizing no longer existed. All the buildings are built this way because someone a long time ago did it this way. The concept of making a building that might be square or oblong, or have a sloping roof has never been contemplated.

These are major differences between the minds of Torrians, Quarians, and others, and Earthlings, differences that must be buried in the genes, maybe in the way each of us evolved. "I'm amazed, Tom, and concerned for all of us." Tanda's mind must be similar to Cor-ah's. She has grasped what I've been thinking.

"I've never heard the word abstract until you brought it up earlier in our relationship, and as soon as you gave me the word, you gave me the meaning of the word. Abstract, theory, concept. These words aren't in our vocabulary and now you have told me why.

"We've been pretty arrogant in our dealings with those from Marq, haven't we? It appears we have been saying, 'you are different from us, therefore, you are less'." Tanda and Rohn-Da had that look of embarrassment on their handsome faces, and I felt as bad as one can.

"I think I understand the answer to one of the questions about how the nether people were able to get here, able to use the proper words and signs, to get past the gate keepers. I'm not a gambling man, Rohn-Da, Tanda, but I'd bet a couple of paychecks that at one time, how many millions of years ago, people on either side of the universal separation were able to travel back and forth, but it was only the nether people who maintained the knowledge. They have an understanding of the past, how it could influence the future, and are using that knowledge to infiltrate our side of the universe.

"Rohn-Da, do you understand fully what I've just said? Be as honest with me as possible, because if you don't I will take the time to teach you." He nodded yes, and I plunged forward. "You must contact Qadroth as quickly as possible and tell him what I just said. He must go back to the beginnings of time, back when the Quarian tribes were venturing into the universe, maybe even before, and learn the real secrets of the universe, the knowledge of Clotero." I actually had sweat on my forehead and could feel wetness on my back and neck. Rohn-Da just grabbed me, surprised the hell out me, and hugged for all he was worth. His little roly-poly body was shaking he was so excited. He knew that he had just learned something. Tanda, who preceded him, smiled indulgently. I felt embarrassed as hell.

"I'm so embarrassed, Tom. Yes, I understand what you've said, and I'll leave immediately. Teach us, Tom. Teach the council. Teach the people of the universe. Humans are not less because of the way their minds work, their ability to understand the abstract make them superior in many ways. You mentioned your calling, well I agree, teaching us will take many years, my friend." He was gone and Tanda took my hand, as Cor-ah has done so many times.

"You're a dear friend. Cor-ah will be here in a moment. Let's have a cup of hot mako and brighten ourselves up a bit. Cor-ah said you made mako for her on Earth. How did you do that?" She led me into her kitchen and thoughts of dorlies and pigglies, and roqua played about my mind. Toad liver.

"I made us coffee, Tanda. It is so similar that it's amazing. Cor-ah made a pot as well. Have some fun with her and tell her I brought her some fudge."

"What is toad liver?   Sometimes, I just don't understand you at all, but I'm in awe, also.   Cor-ah saw your abilities immediately, Tom, and drew strength from you. That's not a normal trait for a Torrian woman.

"Our arrogance has been showing in all its aspects, I'm afraid.   Can you find it in your human heart to forgive?"   I had my arms around this wonderful woman, hugging her as her husband hugged me just moments before.   If I can't live on Torry for the rest of my life, I hope I can bring these people to Earth with me. She wants me to forgive her?

"Forgive?   Tanda, my lovely Tanda.   I have nothing to forgive.   You haven't done anything that calls for forgiveness.   All I've found since I arrived on Torry is love and   sensitivity,   exquisite   compassion.   There   are differences between us, but not differences that would drive our species from each other.   Rather, I've found a need to become closer, to create strong friendship.   As you know, I love your daughter, and I hope you know I love you and Rohn-Da and Tetta as well."   Careful Tom, you'll be crying in a minute.   God, I really do love my new family.   Little Tetta.   I almost hurt her the other night, a hurt that would have gone soul deep.   Now, thank God I might have found a way to help save her and how many other half-nether children on this beautiful little planet.

"These differences are another way in which we have evolved, and in the case of those of us from Earth, evolved with genes from our own ancestors, those of our Quarian cousins, and now we find out, those of the nether people.   If through genetic manipulation we are able to isolate those genes from the nether people that produce the negative aspects of human life, such as hate and bigotry, selfishness, and a desire sometimes to hurt those around us, then we'll be more like you and the people of Torry.   What a wonderful thought that is.

"But, Tanda, we will have to be very careful when we do this genetic manipulation that we don't destroy what is the basis of being human.   There is compassion in humans, there is romance and love, above all, there is the desire to investigate the abstract, the conceptual, to eternally search for something different, something new, and often search for the truth.   We tend to always be seeking, to be on a quest for something; knowledge, beauty, love, danger. Yes, truth.   When a human looks to the horizon, his first thought tends to be something about 'what's over the edge, there?' We tend not to be satisfied with what we have, but wish and strive for more." Yes, that's it isn't it? Search for the truth, strive for more. That is the human characteristic that seems to be missing in these other human forms, this desire to gain something, to learn something, to prove something. We use history and these fine people don't understand history even as a concept.

I could be at any home on Earth where the lady of the house is brewing up a pot of coffee for a visitor, with windows looking out on vistas filled with colorful trees, bushes, flowers, where the husband just left for work and daughters are soon to be home, but of course I'm not. I'm in a circular home, watching an alien build a pot of mako and whose husband just disappeared in thin air to attend a universal council session.   Of course, I'm mad, but my mind simply won't slow down.

"These little quirks are very human today, and they're what make us different from Torrians, or for that matter, most members of the Universal Council. That isn't bad, it's just different. I wouldn't want to be without them myself, because it's these very characteristics that you've found so fascinating.   Let's not be frightened of these differences, Tanda, let's enjoy them and work to make both our species that much better in our own eyes."

That little speech came straight from my heart, and Tanda and I were hugging each other, holding on and rocking back and forth, standing in the middle of her kitchen, mugs of mako on the counter, when it became very apparent we weren't alone.

"Dear Cor-ah. I didn't hear you come in. I'm afraid I've accidentally frightened your mother." Cor-ah was beaming, gave me a kiss on the cheek, hugged her mother, and stepped back to observe her love hugging her mother. Hugs must be a universal language, for in my travels on Earth, and now through space and time, it's the hug that binds people.

"You and mama were so deep in your thoughts, the building could have fallen around you and you wouldn't have known it. I've been standing here for ten minutes, heard every word between you and father and Tom, and you were so attuned to Tom, you didn't even know I was here." That was the source of her beaming smile, and her humor immediately came into play. "You know, a girl shouldn't be jealous of her own mother. And you better not have been kidding about bringing fudge back with you."

That wasn't said in jest, I understood immediately. I better find a damn good outlet for fudge because this girl is earnest in her love of the stuff.

She got serious again, took one of our cups of mako and drained it. "I'm glad I came in when I did. I have a much better understanding of what we're doing now." I outlined what Riba wanted the two of us to do on Toland, and Cor-ah said she had already talked with Riba and understood. Measuring across our own galaxy, the Milky Way as we call it, Marq, as the rest of the universe seems to know it, it covers millions of light years. How big is the galaxy in which Torry exists? Just how far can these people have discussions through their minds? From Marq to wherever the Universal Council meets, and I don't have any idea where that is, is how far? From there to Torry is how far? Can the strength of these minds be that powerful?

"Apparently, my human love, when we lost the ability to understand problems, to be able to think in the abstract, and learned to compartmentalize our minds, this amazing ability, as you put it, became a part of our being. Yes, if Riba wants to say something to me, he simply focuses on that, and I understand. It's not like when we're all sitting together and we all understand what each is saying. This is very personal."

Riba told me something like that when we first met. I remember him saying he resides in my mind, and if I need to talk to him, all I need do is make that known within my own mind. If I wanted one of them right this instant I could ask Riba or Rohn-Da to come here and they would understand. This kind of communication would put the cell phone companies out of business permanently. I'm picturing some of the very selfish humans I've run into not being able to simply not answer a call, or holding mind conversations while a waitress twiddles her thumbs waiting for an order. Funny stuff, Tom, but not why we're here today. Cor-ah was just staring at me, and Tanda was totally confused.

I have to remember to discuss the scientific problems that will flood our thoughts when it comes time to find out about the nether people's genetic codes. I'm not sure the scientific community on Earth would be capable of such a task for humans. In the universe just how many genetic codes might there be? There is another problem that we'll have to work out. How many genetic codes might there be in the nether universe? This might be a huge challenge, and faced by a Universal Council that doesn't understand the concept of history.

"Tom, we are going to have to take each of these problems you're outlining and work them out one at a time." Cor-ah had deep thought lines furrowing across her brow and I knew that she fully understood everything I'd been thinking and discussing. "When we have most of these problems worked out my special human friend, I want you to teach me how to understand history. I want to know."

That smile sent chills through my entire nervous system one more time, and of course, there were other thoughts mingled with the current problems of what to do about the nether people.

Tanda had fixed us each another cup of mako and concluded our get together in a typical Torrian way. "So, you and Cor-ah are discussing children, eh?" Luckily I didn't have a mouthful of hot mako when she said that. Cor-ah just smiled, patted my arm and lowered her eyes slightly, with a definite look of the devil on her face. Tanda smiled, patted my other arm and left the room. There was nothing that I could say. Nothing.

We finished our mako and were talking about what to do when we reach Toland. "We could leave right away, you know. Make our plans after we arrive, and meet with Kantor El, maybe later tomorrow."

"You have an evil mind, Cor-ah." Our trip through that little phone booth was just as fast as the first time, and that hazy thought of being quite mad slipped through my mind. We space danced to the bus station, where we booked our reservation, and slipped into the booth. Before Cor-ah put the token in the machine, she answered my question about my sanity. One more time.

"When one wishes to know one isn't dreaming, sometimes one asks to be pinched. Would you like to be pinched again, Tom? Or maybe spanked?" We arrived on the island at the same time I got my butt pinched, and I caught an evil, wanton look from that beauty. It took little time to get inside our love palace amid tropical breezes. "You have something weighing on your mind, Tom.

Before we completely let ourselves be drowned in love, tell me."

Chapter Eleven

"You even know something I'm thinking before I think it. This crazy thought has been worming around inside my head for several days, even before we went back to Earth. As a human, I have certain thought patterns and ideas that no one else in the universe seems to have, I have this huge desire to learn, to test theories, to develop concepts, to want to think outside the box as we often say.

"Anyway, what if this ability of humans to think in the abstract, to conceptualize, is not from the nether people? If back at the time of Clotero's bringing order to the universe, and establishing life in the various galaxies, what if all forms of thinking beings had this ability, and it is simply the order of evolvement that's changed? The human developed based on the genes of the two species that had been mingled, and this evolvement took a different path than that of many other subspecies. Do you remember me saying we had to take some time, a long time, and sit and discuss this evolution question? I think now is the right time to do it.

"I've been letting this circle around inside my head bone for several days now and I'm getting more and more sure that in reality there aren't any nether people. There may be a nether universe, but I'm almost positive there isn't an invasion of nether people into this universe. Let's just sit here and let our minds contemplate this question of evolution by way of Quarian genes mixing with the various genes of other galaxies and see where it leads us."

I was sitting on the bed, Cor-ah sat down next to me and as she does so often took my hand and held it tightly. "Promise to go slow, Tom. I'm just now learning this idea of conceptual, abstract thinking. But I'm sure I know where you might be going with your thoughts. Do you remember me saying I've never really been afraid, when we were on Earth? It might just be happening again." We did something we had never done before, moved up onto the bed, fully clothed, thank you, and hugged each other. "We have something no one else in the universe has, Tom. Let's put it to good use and solve this damn problem once and for all."

"Close your eyes, Cor-ah and let your mind go free. Don't try to compartmentalize anything, just let your mind be free to act and go in any direction it feels like, and let's see what happens. Free association is what humans call it. Your mind is so quick and your ability to understand complex problems is so tuned to mine, that we might just be able to do this." She closed her eyes, her fingers actually digging into me, but she had a benign look crossing her face, she was so close to what might be called a meditative state that I actually thought she might have done this before.

"In many of our religious teachings on Earth, the concept of free will is at the heart of who we are. There are those who believe that we moved from an understanding of a god and all the universe into what we are because of this thing we call free will. Can you see how a Quarian gene might cause this? Mixing with the genes of maybe a naturally aggressive, or overly egoistic, animal form on Earth, the Quarians set in motion a process that eventually evolved into the human as we know him today. That process is slowly starting to develop in other galaxies. If this is a natural part of evolution, then our two sets of minds will probably not come together in an understanding such as we've been discussing. Cor-ah, I have a struggle right now.

"It may not be possible to close the gate on the nether people because there may not be a gate. The nether people may not be from a twin universe, but rather, the two universes function as one, the separating factor being free will. I wonder if it's an evolutionary process for the concept of free will to spread through the universe. The Shangri La of mind travel, no separation of time and space, will come to an end for all the universe as it has on Earth?"

"You are scaring me again, Tom. I think I know what you're saying, though. Do other members of the Universal Council have or did they have this idea of free will, as you call it, in their past? Was it connected by way of the Quarian genes? Is it a part of all our genes?"

Evolution is a funny thing, and even though Cor-ah has never had a day of education, she is picking up on what I think is the major problem we're looking at. It isn't a problem, it's simply a function of evolution. Maybe the term, "free will" isn't the right one. Maybe we need to get a little deeper definition into the concept. I had to continue because she seemed to be grasping the thought.

"If, as a human, I have developed in certain ways different from species that also sprang from the Quarian Sonneth, and because of the species he chose to mate with had a set of genes that allowed for the human to develop a mind and system of thinking that it would take the rest of the universe untold millions of years to catch up with, the rest of the universe at some time in the future will be like the humans." Her eyes are telling me that she understands exactly what I'm talking about, so I continued.

"Each of the species that Sonneth mated with millions of years ago contributed genes to the Universal Council gene pool, but since there is very little interspecies mating, those genes have not had a chance to blossom into what the human has become. At some point in time, possibly thousands of generations from now, all of us in the universe will have the same types of minds and thoughts. This evolutionary process will not be happening in a specific timetable."

"What you're saying, Tom, there are no nether people. There is no invasion from another universe. Those of us from the other galaxies will become similar to

161

humans from Earth. Tom, does this mean we won't have our lives together? I'm afraid. For the first time in my life, I'm afraid. I mean it this time, Tom. Not like on Earth, but really afraid. Not like with Tetta or with vehicles, but with how my life is going to be. Mama is so worried about Tetta and all I can think about is you and me. Is that being selfish, Tom?" Tears were on her cheeks, she was seriously afraid, and it was my fault. I, yes, the totally nutso Human Tom, did this to the woman he loves. Damn me.

"We're going to be apart, aren't we?" We were lying across the large bed, holding, hugging, touching. I could feel my blood coursing through my veins, partly because I was so close to Cor-ah, but also because now I knew why I was here. I am here to make this transition for other species one that will not tear the universe apart. Some power above mine, above that of the Universal Council saw to it that I would be here, right here, in bed with Cor-ah, knowing what I had to do with the rest of my life.

"No. We won't be apart but we will move through the universe in different ways than those that follow us. It won't be our generation that will be affected, but like Tetta, the process has begun. Her children, and then theirs, will continue until, who knows how many generations down the line, the ability to travel through time and space will not exist, conversations across the universe will end." I had that damn sense of humor working again and Cor-ah gave me a serious poke in the ribs. All I had said to myself was, you will have to learn to ride in a vehicle.

"Regardless, we will be together. On Earth? Maybe. On Torry? Maybe. You won't lose your natural genetic compass, but our children won't be to your standards. I'm afraid we only have tonight, and then we have to go to the Universal Council and make them aware of what is happening. They won't like it, but this isn't something that can be changed. It was put in motion several million years ago by Sonneth at the direction of Clotero."

The arrogance of the Quarian will blossom into full light when we bring these thoughts before the council. Quarians are at the heart of the entire problem and with their superiority complex in question they may find themselves not in control. It is control that has driven the Quarians from the beginning, from the time Sonneth traveled through the universe spreading his seed.

"Something else for us to think about is this question of history or a lack of it and the control that Quarians demand. If you and the other subspecies don't have this concept of understanding your history, why is it that everyone understands what Sonneth did? The only thing that is passed down is how the Quarian tribe brought about the subspecies and how important that is to know. This is right in line with the idea of control of others. Control is the answer to this problem and what I'm seeing right now is scary to me." What just rammed its way through my brain is simply this: I'm not here to find the nether people, I'm here to protect the Quarian image and allow the Quarian to maintain their total control over the subspecies.

"We need to rest a bit, pretty lady, before we continue this. My head hurts."

An evil gleam, sparkling eyes devouring me, and just one comment. "Teach me what happens after our nap."

A nap, alone on a warm summer afternoon is a glorious thing that can bring all the senses back into focus. A nap with an inter-galactic beauty on a tropical isle is just about the epitome of sensational. With all the batteries charged, I spent a couple of long sensuous hours teaching Cor-ah exactly what happens after a nap. "Oh, Tom, I don't understand. Teach me again, Tom." We ate a very late meal, two very tired time and space travelers working on the family of man.   Morning came earlier than it should have. Morning meant we had to go to Council and I had to spread, in one thought the very good news, in another, a devastating blow to the ego of the Quarians.

"You're an evil man.   Evil.   And I love you. We don't have to get up do we? We don't have anywhere to go do we?" Her eyes were half closed, a little smile dancing around inviting lips, and hair tousled properly, all I could do was agree with her. After all, I'm just a lowly human.

If the Quarian gene that created this desire for learning, for wanting to know who we are, why we are, what we are on Earth to accomplish mixed freely with the entities Sonneth encountered on Earth it would explain so much.   If that gene was suppressed some way within the Quarian, it would also explain so much. "Cor-ah, we have said that Torry and Earth are so much alike, our people are so much alike, so obviously compatible," and I got a sock in the ribs on that one, "and all the various people that make up the Universal Council have Quarian genes, then we have our answer.

"My ancestors had genes that mixed with Quarian genes and produced a human being. Your ancestors had genes that mixed with Quarian genes and produced Torrians.   Evolution is going to affect each of the various subspecies based on the original genes and how they mixed with those from the Quarian.   The people from Earth are very much like the people of Torry. Our original ancestors had to have been somewhat similar.   Eventually that Quarian gene is going to allow for an evolution of each subspecies, and in different ways.

"There hasn't been an invasion of nether people. There has been evolution started millions of years ago by Sonneth. Bless his soul." She looked at me with that deep understanding that comes from closeness, and I think we both had the same idea at the same time. This wasn't mind reading on her part, and could not have been on my part.

"How do we tell the Quarians that this evolutionary process isn't a human failure but is because of a Quarian gene that mixes freely.

"Quarians have been dominating the Universal Council, apparently for thousands of generations, but have never given a moment's notice to history and yet Qadroth is aware that he is the 132nd chairman of the council. There are no books, no schools, people have done over and over what was done how many generations ago?" Cor-ah was looking at me again as if for her first time.

"Qadroth, all the Quarians I've ever met seem to feel because it was Sonneth that traveled the universe so long ago that they have the right to be number one." She wasn't smiling. "I had never given that a second's thought until just now, Tom. How will we be able to even broach the subject?"

"That desire to dominate is the gene that allowed the human to evolve differently from other subspecies, it mixed freely with an existing gene and created a human being with desires not found in other areas of the universe. Other subspecies will eventually become more like humans, I'm positive of this." This idea of Torrians and O'nians, and others becoming like humans, that is, selfish, dominating, willing to kill and maim, enslave and make war, is not a pretty picture. Cor-ah was "hearing" everything in my mind.

"The Quarians are almost like that already," she said, and I immediately related to Riba and Qadroth. "I'm right, you're right, and we have to tell them. That won't be fun, my human friend."

We had to pare down our thinking, make sound arguments based on fact, as I pointed out to her, we had to create what might be described on Earth as a scientific paper for publication or for an advanced degree. The Quarians have been dominating the council and all the other subspecies for millions of years, and because of their own egotistical and arrogant nature didn't even realize that the problem that was being encountered was one of their own making.

"How do we tell Qadroth and Riba something like this?" Cor-ah had never had to think outside what was considered natural to a Torrian and the idea of informing the all-powerful Quarians that they were responsible for the way the humans developed and responsible for the way younger Torrians were developing was overwhelming to her. "He will be furious, Tom. Papa has mentioned his temper, saying it frightened him."

"I've seen Riba simply make statements about situations without discussing the consequences with anyone. I can imagine his temper as well. Let's spend at least one more day here, and go back to your house and talk with your mother and father. We need to present a solid front when we meet with the council."

Chapter Twelve

Cor-ah and I had some long discussions about how her life and my life are so different, and we came out knowing more than I could have expected. Our upcoming meeting with Qadroth, Riba, and the council would be very difficult and these next few hours might be our only time alone together for some time. "I'm a little worried about one thing in particular, Cor-ah. Riba seems to know where I am and what I'm doing at all times. Yannow, the gatekeeper seemed to know I was coming to see him. This is not conducive to trust.

"Back home we have laws protecting our privacy, keeping someone from prying into our very private lives, and yet Riba seems to know where you are, where I am, what is transpiring in various places, even understanding private thoughts. Do you have this ability as well?"

"No. That is purely Quarian. No other subspecies is able to do what you have described. I've never given it any thought before, but it is a form of mind control, isn't it?" She had the frown of worry across that broad face and she knew she had just opened another set of circumstances that separates all the subspecies from the original Quarian species. "This is how they have maintained their position all these generations, knowing what others are thinking and learning and attempting to stop it. They thought that you would simply bow to their thoughts. Tom, you are in danger right now. You are about to blow their conspiracy into shreds. They thought that a human brought before the council would simply act as the other subspecies do, and they didn't understand the human mind at all."

That beautiful little girl just nailed the problem. "I thought you didn't understand conceptual thinking, dear heart. We will be walking into a fire storm when we go before the council. All the Quarians will know what we're

167

bringing and none of the other subspecies members will have a clue. I hope your mother and father are as fast on their feet with their minds as you are because we are all at a bit of risk right now.

"You have said that you would tell me about this ability of yours to flit about through time and space, I think it's time."

"It is time." She was wearing a tropical print blouse with white shorts. Those vivid eyes were alive with color and actually sparkled as she danced across the sand at the edge of the lagoon on Toland. "I want a promissory note from you, I mean this Tom, a legal letter that you will keep me in fudge for the rest of my life if I tell you my deep, dark secrets."

"So you have now learned a human trait called hostage bargaining, eh, little devil?" We were chasing each other across the beach, into the shallow waters, back onto the beach, and we caught each other, of course. "You win, kiddo, all the fudge you can handle is yours. How do you do it?"

"Like this," she said, and we were standing in her front yard back on the mainland. "See? Easy, isn't it?" She danced into the house laughing and taunting me, mercilessly. Oh, she's evil, I was thinking when she came back out munching on the last piece of fudge left from our earth visit. "I simply let my mind know where I wanted to be, that I wanted to bring you with me, and here we are. Now, where is that letter, my dear soon-to-be husband?"

It's just not fair, but I better get used to it. I'm going to be with this little vixen for a long time and she will always be in command, there's no doubt. "You know our kids won't be able to do that." We found ourselves changing from the frivolity of vacation to the seriousness of the situation and Cor-ah got right to the point.

"Actually the way we were talking about this, this morning, they will probably have about the same abilities as Tetta or maybe that Kantor-El on Toland. We don't know if Kanto-El's father had full ability as I do, or whether the younger man might even be a third generation with limited ability. Maybe that's why Tetta has much less mind abilities than anyone else in the family. If this ability is evolutionary as we think it is, it might be something that can be learned to a degree.

"Do you remember telling me that you thought earth people probably had these same abilities but grew away from them through an evolutionary process? And do you remember telling me you thought you picked up on Riba getting ready to send you to Yannow?

"Well, let's just see what we can do. I've already won all my fudge, so let's just see." She got very serious again and we went into the house, sat at the dining room table and said it was time for a cup of mako. "Go ahead, Tom, make a pot of mako."

I closed my eyes and concentrated on putting the ingredients together to make a pot of coffee and of course nothing happened. I took it one step at a time.

Put water in pot. Nothing.

Put mako in pot. Nothing.

Again. Nothing. "I don't think I'm doing it right, Cor-ah." She squeezed my hand, gave me a little peck of a kiss and spoke very softly.

"You will never have the ability, Tom. What you will have is the knowledge that it can be done, and when it is time to move from one time or space to another, you will eventually know it is coming. And that is about all."

That isn't what I wanted to hear, you know, as a doctor might say I'm sick, or a cop giving a ticket. I knew that was going to be the answer, I just didn't want to hear it.

"We have talked about subjects that you have indicated you had never heard of and yet you talk about them as if you had studied the subject. Cor-ah, there are no

169

books, no schools, no history or science that is studied and yet we have discussed in detail the possibility of evolution, its consequences, the theories of how all this has come about and you seem fully aware.   How is that possible?" This one had been playing around in my head for some time, here we go again, days, weeks, months, who knows what time means?   Still sitting at the table in that warm kitchen atmosphere, a fresh cup of mako at hand, Cor-ah gave me a long look, deep into my soul.

"I'm sitting right here, Tom, right next to you, you can reach out and touch me anytime you wish," and she reached over and gave me a little peck on the cheek, "but I think I also exist in your mind.   Don't stop me yet, I'm actually being aggressive in my thinking here, like you do sometimes, conceptualizing for the first time in my life." She was amazing herself, it seems.   Her mind was my mind, and we were thinking this thing out together.   Riba had told me he existed in my mind, but he didn't understand the concept of conceptual thinking, and Cor-ah is doing it.

"When we talk," she had slowed her speech down, thinking as she spoke, something Torrians have never done in my presence, "I understand things as you tell me about them.   I'm inside your mind, with a complete understanding of something I've never even heard of before.   Concepts, realities, sciences even are things I had never given a moment's nod to, and yet when we talk, when we discuss these ideas, I have a full understanding of them.

"I've never heard the words evolution or conceptual or abstract until you spoke them, but in an instant I knew what we were discussing.   I understand fully Tetta's situation because I understand evolution.   How is that possible?   It's my turn to ask these questions, Tom.   How, why are we able to do this?"

I hadn't realized it, but we were holding hands so tightly that my fingers were beginning to cramp. We have reached another level, one beyond what Riba and I have, one that can give us the ability to teach entire galaxies what they will need in order to come full circle in this evolutionary mush pile. Sitting at the table, looking into each other's eyes, holding tightly onto reality and at the same time allowing our minds to expand into infinite space, time, futures, pasts - multiple realities is what this entire process has been about. "I know why I'm here, now, Cor-ah. It's you. We will do things no two people in this universe have ever conceived of doing."

Someone has to bring the rest of the universe up to speed. Now there is an egotistical, arrogant, human thought. "That's right, we have to create a history that can be taught to future generations. Some of the subspecies will dive in feet first," and I got a good giggle out of that, "and others, probably led by the Quarians, will object and not participate, but that is our mission." I'm a nut-case from Earth and I'm in love with an Aphrodite from another galaxy and I'm going to save the universe. Yeah, right.

"You're so funny sometimes. More mako, nut-case?" The laugh was as real as anything I've ever heard but was followed immediately by an awareness of what had to be done. "What do we tell mama and dad?"

Of course, there was still the Universal Council to take into consideration. Those people are not going to be pleased with what we have to tell them. "The Quarians I'm afraid will be the least pleased of the bunch, my little trouble maker. They are so damn proud of themselves and so willing to call the rest of the universe their subspecies, it might be dangerous when we tell them it is their genome that is creating this evolutionary process to alter what they believe is perfect.

"The human genome was the first to change as that gene's work was done not too long after development.

171

Whatever animal or very early humanoid it was that the Quarian had relations with was probably a little bit aggressive to start with, and the Quarian's feelings of superiority led to what we now call the human from Earth, from the Marq system. And all the other subspecies have that Quarian gene that eventually will lead to a form of being more like the human than the Quarian. What they created so many millions of years ago is slowly taking form through the natural evolutionary process. No, my little pet, they will not like to hear what we are going to tell them.

"Can you let your mother and father know we need to talk to them without Riba and Qadroth knowing it?"

"I'm not sure just how closely Riba and Qadroth monitor what you in particular and papa do? I have already asked mama and dad to join us here, so they should arrive shortly. This is really going to be tricky, isn't it? Just getting ready to attend council will be very difficult."

As I picked up my cup, Rohn-Da and Tanda materialized in the kitchen and sat down with us. I can't get the picture of a large woman, back home, materializing in an awkward place and the confusion and chaos that would cause. Humans would not behave well if we had this ability.

"Tom, I'm glad you and Cor-ah are back from Toland. There has been lots of talk around the council about what might be happening. I'm afraid that Riba is very angry right now. What did you and Cor-ah find out from that Kantor-El?"

"We never went to see him, papa," Cor-ah jumped in quickly. "Listen to what Tom and I have worked out, and let us know what you think. Mama, it's very important that you listen as well. It appears that Riba, Qadroth, and other Quarians spend a great deal of time prying into our private lives, and what Tom has discovered could lead to a dangerous situation.

"Please wait until we are completely through outlining this problem before you speak, and then, we will want to discuss the answers in detail." Cor-ah was one strong lady to talk to her parents that way, but they must have known that for years. With cups of fresh mako at hand, looks of consternation on Tanda's and Rohn-Da's faces, I launched into a dissertation on what Cor-ah and I had come up with on Toland. It took at least a half hour to get it all out, and Rohn-Da looked like a whipped puppy when I got through.

"I've actually feared something like this in the past Tom, but didn't have any idea how to put it into words or even who to discuss it with. The idea of nether people gave the Quarians, in particular Qadroth the means to have even more control over the council and over various aspects of our lives.

"It's funny, isn't it, that Riba didn't know exactly what you would come up with?" The chubby little guy gave the appearance of being defeated, but a quick look Tanda's way, and I understood. He was giving in to the stronger of the pair and she got right to the point.

"I think we must all attend the next meeting, Tom. You will make a presentation such as what you just did for Rohn-Da and me, and Cor-ah, who understands far more than we do, will back you up. But with Rohn-Da, a council member and me a representative of our Torry government, they will have to be careful how they react. We do have rights and I for one will insist that things be above board." There was the Torrian woman in perfect form and I could see Rohn-Da straighten up a little bit. He'll be fine, I told myself, and could almost feel Cor-ah saying the same thing.

Chapter Thirteen

One or more of the council members had apparently been listening in to what Cor-ah and I had been discussing on Toland and at her home, something that Riba had told me more than once was forbidden. Forbidden by those not on the council, eh? There were rules for the subspecies that may not have been rules for Quarians, I believe and this was one of them. What I was wondering now was just how much council members from the other subspecies knew and how they found out about it. By knowing that we might understand what our position was going to be, whether we had friends at the table, or whether everyone would be against us. I could feel myself tensing up, could feel eyes penetrating into my soul.

There were many sets of what might be called the evil-eye, giving us a stern warning on what might be coming. Qadroth did not welcome us, did not say anything, simply started in on me. Cor-ah smiled benignly at him and at Riba, gave her papa a big smile, and held tightly to my hand. I could feel the tension she felt. She knew everything those at the table were thinking and all I could do was guess. I bet my guess was pretty accurate.

After drinking endless cups of mako, Rohn-Da and Tanda said they felt sure they understood what the problem was and couldn't conceive of how to correct what was happening. "It seemed right when we thought the problem was an invasion of nether people from a separate universe, didn't it?" Rohn-Da said. "Now we're facing a conspiracy that may have begun at the beginning of our time and actually involves those we thought were our friends and neighbors." The pudgy little guy looked whipped, Tanda was crying softly, and Cor-ah was scowling. She was angry, and I think this is the first time I have seen a Torrian angry. I knew she had a temper, I'd seen part of that, but this was deeper, a personal anger.

"Mama, I think we should all go to the council meeting. Papa, you're a member of the council, I'm accepted as being able to attend regularly, and Mama, you have a position here on Torry that would certainly let you sit in on a meeting. This is going to be very nasty, and probably dangerous, and we must go to protect Tom, to protect little Tetta, and most of all, to end this conspiracy of domination." She was working on her speech to the council, I thought, and using arguments to her parents and me that would come out later.

Rohn-Da perked up when Cor-ah spoke, enough that I felt he would be okay at the meeting, Tanda was worried, but was so very strong, much like her oldest daughter, that I knew she would do fine. To be truthful, I was worried about me. My old Earth style temper might flare up and that would not go over well. We'll let them show their anger and we'll show our contempt through knowledge is what I told my new family. It only took a flash of time to arrive at the meeting.

Qadroth had none of his eloquent presence with him as he spoke to me. "So, human Tom, you say you are coming to help us fend off an attack from the nether universe, but in reality you are in a conspiracy with those from Torry to disband the Universal Council, to make unfounded claims against us, and to belittle our beliefs." Qadroth was shaking he was so angry, and for the first time I was really able to see what I had been thinking for some time. The Quarian mind is positive that Quarians are the leaders of the universe and everyone else had better understand this.

I could remember when I was first brought before the council and I was sure that I had been threatened by this man. His soft, very political approach caught me off guard and I allowed myself to fall into his trap. He was controlling from the first moment I met him, and Riba, that old Aztec was his henchman. Qadroth had the makings of a conspirator that could run for public office or control a criminal organization. Smooth when necessary, fearful and dangerous when challenged.

From the moment we arrived, it was the Quarians at the table that were attempting to stare us down, to put on their game-face as athletes like to say, and looking around the large room as Qadroth attempted to abuse me with his wit and wisdom, it was Riba giving the hardest stare. Riba had almost become a person in my mind recently, but at this moment, he was the farthest thing from being anything other than that horrid old entity I first met.

"No, Qadroth," I started to respond to the chairman of the council, but Rohn-Da stood up, pointed a finger at Qadroth and called him a fake and cheat.

"It is important that this council listen to what Tom has to say. He came to us in all humility, I remember that first time, and you and this council begged him to help with what we thought was an invasion from another universe.

"Qadroth, as the ranking member of the Torrian representatives, I demand that this council hear what Tom has to say. I demand it." Rohn-Da was shaking. His whole body was spreading a language of anger and it seemed that many of the other subspecies in the room were nodding in his favor. There must have been many conversations going on that I would love to know about. I wonder if Rohn-Da had had an opportunity to spread his thoughts before he made them public here. Did he talk to others before we arrived? Damn, I wish I could listen in to some of these conversations.

This was not going to be an easy Sunday afternoon family gathering. Rohn-Da, that wonderfully pudgy, soon-to-be father-in-law was ready to do battle, and his weapons were good ones. Torrian women were supposed to be the stronger of the sexes and if what I was seeing was a weaker of the sexes I don't ever want to totally inflame the passions of Tanda or Cor-ah.

"You have broken several council edicts, Qadroth, spying on my daughter, lying to the council, and now, accusing a man whose only function has been to help us, of working against us. It is you, Qadroth and all the other supercilious Quarians who have worked against the Universal Council. Let Tom speak, for what he says will be how we will live for the next several thousand generations. He has a mind far superior to anything at this council, a mind that understands the concept of a problem, and a mind that can take that problem and work it to a satisfactory conclusion."

I've known Rohn-Da for how long? I don't know what time means anymore, but I have known that man long enough to know that his passions run deep and true. Cor-ah was ready to cry she was so excited by her father's outburst, and I wanted to stand and cheer on the one hand and hide under the table on the other.

Representatives from numerous subspecies were in the room, probably close to one hundred, maybe more, and the Quarians were seriously outnumbered but with their superior mind strength compared to the other subspecies, they felt they had the advantage. Well, there is that superiority complex one more time. Cor-ah nudged me, almost poked me, if you will, and I prepared myself to stand up and be heard.

The floating lamps highlighted beads of sweat on foreheads all over the chamber, I know I was sweating profusely, but interestingly, Riba and Qadroth were not. My mind saw it immediately. Right there is the conspiracy, right there are where the problems exist. Qadroth and Riba were working in concert and I wonder how long it will be before anyone else sees this. Of course, with me just thinking, it puts the thought into the ether and maybe some of these other members of the council will pick up on it.

"Qadroth," I said, and I was not tenuous at all, rather bold, I felt, and got right to the point. "I have been studying this problem that currently faces the Universal Council, and have reached several conclusions I would like to discuss with the Council." The old cliché, "if looks could kill" went through my mind, but I knew I had to continue. "To prove the theories that Cor-ah and I have worked out will take medical examination but I believe we are right.

"When Sonneth and those with him moved through the various galaxies creating what you call subspecies, he planted the genes of the Quarians into the gene pools of those he inseminated, thus mixing a specific genome of each new subspecies. In some cases, in many cases, apparently, the dominant genes did not take hold immediately but sat and brewed for very long periods of time. In other cases, on Earth in particular, one of the Quarian genes became dominant and what has transpired is what is called a human today."

The rumbling was instantaneous as many members of the council started mind-talking amongst themselves. One thing I learned at our very first meeting was how to put a stop to that and I simply let go with total abandonment. Cor-ah felt it coming and disengaged her mind, but none of the others on the council did. I thought about everything from baseball to love making to the sinking of the Titanic to how many apples it really took to make a fine pie on the one hand or a jug of jack on the other. Within moments, I had that council begging me to stop. Even Rohn-Da was holding his head, but there was a grand smile on his broad face.

Tene, the Sarcathian we had visited Yannow with spoke up. "Tom, I have felt all along that you were doing something other than trying to find the nether people. Did you make your conclusion before you investigated?" That's a nasty little thought, you pip-squeak, but I answered him with my own personal brand of dignity.

"Tene, as Qadroth and other Quarians know, my human mind works somewhat similar to theirs. They do not have the ability to think out a problem, only recognize one. I found the concept of nether people very real when we first began our investigation, and remember Tene, you were part of that investigation. But since you are unable to conceptualize a problem it was up to me to discover what was really taking place."

I hit a nerve with Qadroth and Riba indicating that they probably knew the answer to the problem well before I did. The Quarian mind simply would not grasp that the problem was theirs, but create some other way of addressing it. Create the nether people and then hope that some dumb human could be coerced into going along with the gag. Those two were seething and I know they were also doing some planning on what to do with me and my Torrian colleagues.

At least I had the council's attention again and continued. "There is no one that will disagree when I say that the Quarian is naturally domineering, demands a certain amount of respect, and can be slightly aggressive when provoked." As I looked around the table I caught many there holding back little smiles, nodding to one another, even showing a bit of obvious glee. I was startled though when Cor-ah followed my thoughts with her own.

"Tom also just described a human if you didn't pick up on that. Humans have evolved from the mixing of Quarian and an animal or original humanoid that roamed Earth millions of years ago, and that entity was probably just as domineering, just as aggressive, just as demanding of respect as Sonneth." There was almost open rebellion at this point and I had a hard time getting back control. Qadroth and Riba sat very still, glaring at the two of us, but not attempting to stop me. It hit me then that they were waiting for others on the council to take up the challenge, and Tene's attempt was a disaster. I decided to go for the heart.

"It is that one little Quarian gene that is causing the trouble today, not an infestation of people from a nether universe. It will take many thousands of generations, but eventually all of us in the universe will be like me. Like humans. More than likely it has already begun in other galaxies. We have proof that it is happening in the Torry system. Little Tetta, youngest daughter of Rohn-Da and sister to Cor-ah is an example of what will be taking place.

"Tetta isn't able to use her mind quite as nimbly as Rohn-Da or Cor-ah, still far superior to anything I could do, and it seems Tetta's biological half-brother, one Kantor-El has the same problem. It is a natural evolvement of the Quarian gene becoming dominant. What was thought to be a human trait that allowed those Quarians who have dominated this universal council for all these thousands of generations to keep Earth and the human race out of the council will soon spread to every subspecies in the universe." There was immediate bedlam.

Interestingly, it wasn't aimed at Cor-ah and me, but rather a spontaneous debate had broken out between representatives of various galaxies and the Quarians in attendance. The Quarians were beside themselves, defending their rightful place as head of the universe. They were losing the debate and the battle and if Qadroth wanted to maintain any kind of order he had to act immediately. He knew I wasn't going to work my mind magic on the council. That's when we got the real surprise of the day.

Riba stood up, glaring fiercely, first at me, then at the council members still ranting, then at Cor-ah. It became immediately clear that Qadroth was not the leader of the universal council, Riba was. The old Aztec, that man with no sense of humor but who could dance and drink wine from time to time, was the boss and there was no doubt.

"This session is over."   A simple pronouncement, and it was accepted by all but four. Cor-ah, Rohn-Da, Tanda, and I were not ready to quit. I planned to tell the council how I could help make this major transition a workable one, how I could devise history books and education, how this would be a wonderful learning experience. I never got the first word out of my mouth and found myself lying flat on the floor in my little Virginia City apartment.

"No! This is wrong, Riba, no." I was crying, I was so angry I would have let all the human aggression in me beat the hell out of that little creep, I wanted Cor-ah, I didn't want to lose my new family. "No!" I cried again. I pounded the floor, I kicked furniture, I tore the bedclothes off the bed, and I wanted to break everything I saw. I stormed around the apartment cussing like I had never cussed in my life, and finally wore myself out. That temper tantrum would have been best seen by the council, but wasn't, of course.

As I stood a chair upright, there was Riba, standing in my living room, glaring at me with more than anger in his beady little eyes.   "You bastard, you better defend yourself," and I threw a roundhouse right, bad aim, but generally at his left temple. He danced aside and with mind energy alone forced me to sit down.

"Human Tom, you and the entire human race are banned for eternity from membership in the Universal Council. Moreover, you will not ever be allowed to have contact with any person from any other subspecies for the rest of your life." It was only the strength of his mind that kept him alive at that point for I would gladly have torn him into shreds of Quarian detritus.

"You will never keep Cor-ah and I apart, Riba. You and your superior Quarian bastards can roast in hell, but I will be back with Cor-ah." He lifted his chin in an arrogant display of superiority and vanished.   I was screaming at him as he disappeared, and I had a horrible feeling in the deepest pit of my stomach that he was going to be proved right, that I would never see Cor-ah again.

This isn't the time to give up, and I let my mind slow down, I needed full self-control, I got back to thinking straight, not with uncontrolled anger, and knew that Cor-ah and Tanda would be able to hear me, would know where I am, and would follow through where I was denied the opportunity. The other subspecies had to be made to understand the Quarian conspiracy. "Now is not the time to rant and rave, Tom my boy, but to do some serious planning. I can do this, and I have friends in high places." I had to smile at that arrogant thought and it allowed me to understand what to do.

I needed a good night's sleep, but of course, I tossed and turned the whole time, arguing with Qadroth, with Riba, making love with Cor-ah, even drinking beer with Rohn-Da. The answer to the entire problem would come by way of making the other subspecies members of the council understand the concept of history and then how they have been led and controlled for generations. That is my task.

In the morning, I made a pot of coffee, tried to pretend it was Mako, packed my Jeep and headed for Silver Peak and that special little cave. I knew in my heart that it would be useless, but one must try. My camp was up and I went to the cave, sat in the sand and made the sign that Riba had taught me. I was calling Yannow, I was calling the Yeti, but nothing happened. I wiped the sand clean and made the sign again, but Yannow had been given his orders by the Quarian boss, and I was not to be able to travel through time and space.

Is this what happened so many thousands of years ago? Is this how the human race has been denied all the universe offers? Some arrogant Quarian simply said, 'you can't be a member of this group' and it was all over? The

182

humans of hundreds of thousands of years ago probably were not aware of the compounded loss that followed.

As I sat in camp, getting ready to head back home in defeat another thought crossed my mind. Maybe none of this ever happened. Maybe I am just as loony as I have thought so many times. My mind snapped that day in the heat and I have been suffering from a mental breakdown ever since. "I wonder what day this is." I said that out loud to myself, and didn't have any way of checking. I know what day it was when I first met Riba, when that vicious heat broiled my brain, so what day is today?

Am I in love with a woman who is a figment of a mentally deranged man? Did I not make love with a woman that I want to be with for the rest of my life? My God, I am mad as mad can be. I'm a puddle of warm jelly boiling in the sun and none of this ever happened.

It was a long slow drive, 250 miles worth, back to the Comstock, back to an empty apartment, one that should have been filled with love. And fudge. I dawdled, stopped at every little turn in the road, did everything I could not to have to face that empty hole, a hole filled with black hate, filled with yearning for one more moment with Cor-ah. I stopped at a little wayside store and bought a newspaper and found out that I have been traveling about the universe for more than a month. A month of visits to Toland, to Council, to Torry, back to Earth a time or two, and I'm not mad. That dirty bastard must have been keeping track of us all the time, understanding and knowing all along that we were right. Then the other thought, none of this ever happened. But I know it is happening.

What will they do to Cor-ah and Rohn-Da? I've never felt as helpless as I did when I finally parked the old Jeep and climbed the stairs to my rooms. About half way up I turned around, went out onto the street, and into Cor-ah's favorite Virginia City business and bought half a pound of fudge. "This is for you, babe," and headed home.

As I put the key into the lock, the door opened and I was looking into the broad smiling face of Rohn-Da. He grabbed me and hugged, hugged some more, and we sat down at the kitchen table. "Coffee, my friend?" He smiled and shook his head.

"I brought some Mako," and a pot of steaming Mako was sitting on the table with two recently washed cups. I didn't wash them. "I have a mission, Tom, and one I dread but I must do it. It might mean I will lose my daughter. Will you listen?" I agreed at once, and he reached across the table and took my hand, much like Cor-ah would have done.

"I'm not mad, Rohn-Da. Listen to me, I'm not mad." I wanted to dance, sing, pick up my fine little Torrian friend and whirl around the room. His look of astonishment made me settle down immediately. "I'm sorry, but you know how humans are. What is this terrible thing you are here to tell me?"

"Because of my status on the council they could not keep me from exerting my will. The Quarians were exactly as you said they would be. I have a plan, however." My mind was going a thousand miles an hour because I thought I knew what that plan was going to be. I was so close to the edge of my chair I almost fell off it and Rohn-Da finally got me calmed down enough that he could get a word in.

Rohn-Da was as anxious as I and could hardly control himself as he spoke. "There is considerable confusion among the many galaxies in the council and the Quarians are doing what they can to maintain absolute control, but they are losing. I have taken it on myself to spread your thoughts through the council and Cor-ah has been doing the same. It is chaotic, to say the least, with Quarians continuing to interpose their thoughts into ours.

"I don't know how you came to realize what the problem was, I'll never be able to think like you do, but I am getting the word out. Riba and Qadroth are trying to keep all the various subspecies from being able to travel, particularly to Earth. In some cases it is working, but won't with me.

"I can get Cor-ah here, Tom. Tanda is positive that is what I should do. It could mean we will never see either of you again. If I do this, Riba and Qadroth will try to have me thrown off the council, that I can count on, but they will also take revenge on my family by never allowing us to come here or allowing you to come there."

"The dirty bastards," I said. They intended to hurt that beautiful little family because I did what they asked in the first place. I discovered the truth in the Nether World Invasion. Now this wonderful extended family of mine has to pay for it. I can't tell Rohn-Da to give up his daughter. I would never be able to say that to Tanda. Little Tetta might not be able to understand why her sister is never coming home again. "Damn that little Aztec. Rohn-Da, I don't know what to say. I don't know.

"Just a minute. I might know after all." I almost heard the gears click into place as I thought about them losing Cor-ah, of me losing the biggest fight of my life, of Quarians having so much control over every single piece of life. "Rohn-Da, what you're saying is what they want you to believe. How is it possible for the Quarian species to have that kind of control? Your mind is very strong, you say you came here because you are a member of the council, but how could that be? If you can be here, anyone can be." My poor old worn out brain was in overdrive with no gas in the tank. "Think about this for a minute. How would a Quarian, regardless of which one, have the power to deny everyone in the universe something that is part of your basic genome? It can't be, Rohn-Da. It simply can't be. Go back to Torry, my wonderful papa-to-be and bring Cor-ah here. Don't even hint that she won't be able to go anywhere ever again. I know I'm right on this.

"Listen, some of the other members of the council believe that they can't do something because they have been told they can't. Do you understand?" He nodded that he thought he did and I went right on talking. "Qadroth and Riba are very strong and they have convinced the least of the council members that they will not be able to do something. It is nonsense. You just did, not because you are a member of the council but because you can. You don't believe in the superiority of the Quarian mind. You must spread that word, force some of these people to try to do something that Qadroth has told them they can't do.

"I think you will find many of those subspecies members will not want to try, they are convinced of Quarian superiority, but some will try. Let them know you have been here, had a meeting with me, tell them that I am willing to work with the council to bring about an orderly change. Make them understand the concept of history, what it means to them, what it can mean to their future." I was in a full rant by this time and Rohn-Da was sitting silently, letting me go on and on. He was taking it all in. He was close to understanding as much as Cor-ah was.

"Oh, and wait just a sec." I ran into the living room and grabbed that little white bag filled with fudge. "Bring this to my baby." All of the ideas of Quarian control reached the pinnacle with Rohn-Da's comments about no one being able to travel because they said so. Every subspecies has the Quarian genes that created the subspecies in the first place. The Quarians don't have the ability to simply say no.

Riba could tell me no simply because I couldn't in the first place, and the Quarians do have a certain amount of control over the gate keepers, Yeti and friends, and that would control me, but certainly not a Torrian or a Sarcathian. "I'll bet you a tankard of ale my friend, that Qadroth and Riba told the other subspecies that they could no longer travel through time and space and those

simpletons simply believed what they were told.   Spread
the word, Rohn-Da, that the Quarians are wrong."

He reached out and took my hand again, smiled, his
face filled with love and sadness all at the same time, and
vanished.   Within ten seconds Cor-ah was sitting in that
chair, holding my hand, bawling like a baby, splashing
kisses all over me, and I was doing the same back.   We
didn't let go of each other for more than an hour as we
moved from the kitchen table to the living room couch,
eventually flopping down on the bed, never being able to
talk, just hug and smile and cry and blubber.

We spent the next couple of hours discussing what
all of this meant.   "We certainly know we were right about
our theories.   I guess this idea of attempting to create
universal education systems is out of the question.   And I
won't be able to visit the old people's sites to learn about
their rock writing.   And you'll have to learn how to make
coffee from scratch, I guess."

"Papa told me what you said about the Quarians
trying to keep everyone in their control and I agree.   It is
part of their overall arrogance that they believe that.   I'll bet
they are wrong as hell."

Whoa, that's twice you've used a human cuss word.
Better be careful, little one.

"Let's find out," she said, jumping up and running
into the kitchen.   "See?"   She handed me a cup of Mako
that fast.   "Our kids may not be able to travel like I do,
Tom, but I still have one very strong mind."

That's when I decided it was time to put that mind
to a full test.   "Wait, Cor-ah.   Rohn-Da and I discussed the
Quarians not being able to control every single thing in the
universe.   We agreed that more than likely some of the
subspecies believe they can't travel, but that in reality, all
subspecies except, of course, us humans, still have the
ability to travel through time and space.   I'll tell you what,

you little vixen, let's prove it.   Let's go visit your mama and papa.

"What did you do, bring mako with you?"

"Well, you sent fudge, I brought mako."   We drank a cup, she looked at me and said, "let's just find out how much power these Quarians actually have.   Take my hand, hot shot and hang on tight."   I closed my eyes.   I'm just a big old baby at heart and I knew something really bad was going to happen.   Like Riba showing up, but when I opened my eyes, Cor-ah and I were sitting at the kitchen table on Torry.

"And so the revolution begins, human Tom."   She just smiled, jumped in my lap and gave me about the finest kiss I've ever had in my life.   Tanda broke up the party.

"Rohn-Da doubted your theory, Tom, but Cor-ah never did.   Welcome home.   Qadroth is at council along with Rohn-Da and the other subspecies and Riba is going about the universe trying to kick everyone off the council.   You and Cor-ah need to go to council and support all the subspecies that are in revolt over the Quarian conspiracy to own the universe."

"I think papa would be very proud of you, Tom.   Are you ready for another screaming match?"   Cor-ah was picking up more and more human ways and I love it.   I wanted to say "shazam", but held that back for another time.   Just ending up at council in a blink is enough to scare the hell out of me.

Chapter Fourteen

"First things first, Qadroth, we don't need any more theatrics. I'm not here to create trouble, I'm here to help, which is what was first discussed around here." He had swelled up and was ready to start attacking the moment Cor-ah and I showed up at the council table. I looked around the large auditorium, saw many faces not believing what they were seeing. "Many of you are asking, 'how did the human get here? He was banned from travel.' Well, my friends, the Quarians believe they have total control over every aspect of life in this universe, but obviously they don't.

"Were you told you could only come to council, nowhere else? Were you told that you would lose your council seat if you defied Qadroth and Riba? Do you see me standing before you, supposedly banned, and standing with my soon-to-be wife, Cor-ah, one that was banned, and my soon-to-be-father-in-law Rohn-Da, threatened with losing his council seat? Do you?"

I had my fists doubled up, I was scowling as only a tired old writer can scowl. I was not just challenging Qadroth, I was challenging every soul sitting in those council chambers. My shoulders were set as straight edges and I was defying everything they had held as being the truth as decreed by Clotero himself. What a scene it was, because other subspecies were challenging Quarians for the first time that any of them knew. Little Tene, so obviously the puppy dog of Qadroth, was trying to defend the Quarian dictatorship and was losing badly while Qadroth himself looked defeated in all respects.

Heads swiveled, mind talk raged, Cor-ah and Rohn-Da smiled, Qadroth appeared confused, and our point had been made. "It's time to start thinking in a different manner," I said, again catching everyone by surprise. "This

189

universal council should be led by the most astute among you, not by what we call on Earth, "control freaks". This would be a dictatorship on Earth and it should be universal in nature. All that are sentient beings in the universe should have an opportunity to be represented at council and the council leadership should be open to all."

Cor-ah stood up and looked directly at Qadroth as she said, "I don't think you're qualified to be the leader of this council. I think we need to create a new form of leadership, a committee of leaders, maybe with one person as chairman, and that committee should be elected based on their qualifications."

Wow, Cor-ah, where did you get all that? She really caught me off guard with that little speech, and she had more to say.

"This committee should be made up of various subspecies not dominated by any particular one. If we are going to move forward in history, and really be honest with ourselves, we must take control of how our lives are governed. We need to know our history, we need to know how and why things work. Our children shouldn't grow up only knowing what the Quarians have placed in their heads. They need to be able to expand their learning, and we need to expand our thinking." I'm not sure that was understood, since there was no such thing as history, teaching, learning. I have my work cut out for me. A history of the universe and these people don't know who the last leader of this council was.

"There is so much available in this universe that we know nothing about. I've been to Earth, have you? Other than coming to council, have you been to other galaxies and other planets other than your own? Do you know what it feels like to have a completely unique thought or idea? This is how we will expand and make this universal council exactly what its name implies."

That created the havoc it was intended to do and Cor-ah sat down, looked me right in the eye and smiled and smiled and smiled. You little trouble maker, I do love you. "I know what you have been doing, Cor-ah. You have been probing my mind, learning about things like history and management. You are a little devil, my love, and one that will be a masterful leader someday soon." She gave me another one of those dazzling smiles, telling me that I was right. It was fun to watch as the various council members moved about, discussing points with first this group then the next, glancing from time to time at Qadroth (for his blessing?), wondering whether the old phony would explode in anger. Cor-ah had said, "let the revolution begin," and she fired a mighty first volley.

Less than a minute passed before Qadroth finally exploded, the nasty side of the old snake oil salesman in full view of everyone. No longer this tall, dignified leader of the universal council, the once elegant Qadroth now was an angry old man who was being displaced by those he once fully controlled. As with control freaks everywhere, whether in bad marriages or as political despots, Qadroth struck out immediately at anyone around him, not caring who might get hurt, only insisting on, nay, demanding, his rightful place as leader.

At first, he stood as tall as possible and said, loudly, of course, "This council session is adjourned." Very few heard him and those that did paid no attention, which frustrated the man even more. Cor-ah glanced at me, showing just a touch of fear on that beautiful face but still standing in defiance of Qadroth. The old man shouted obscenities, words that would have made gang bangers in Los Angeles blush, and raged about the room, condemning everyone, screaming insults, flinging his robes about, almost tearing his hair out, that long, silver, wavy hair he apparently has been so proud of all this time.

Cor-ah, still standing, put her hands on her hips, thrust her chin out, smiled at the fallen leader and said, "No, Qadroth, this session is not adjourned," and every internal and loud voice stopped. All eyes were on Cor-ah. "We have business to attend to. We need to create a new set of rules, a new way of doing business, name new leaders, and move into the future while understanding the past. It is time for Quarian control of this council to end." Cor-ah looked long and hard around the room and found virtually everyone waiting for something they couldn't perceive of just minutes ago. They were looking at a new leader, understood Cor-ah was their new leader, and she did, too. There was a determination in her eyes, her face, her mouth, her words that few if any of the other subspecies had ever heard from someone who was not Quarian.

"As of this minute, I am taking control as an interim chairwoman and it is time for us to get down to some serious business. We need to create a committee to work to build a true universal council, so let's start now. Work among yourselves and bring me a committee we can work with to recreate what should have been all along." That is the true Torrian woman, that is what Tanda meant when she said she would have been too strong to sit at council.

Cor-ah looked over at me, scared on the one hand, in charge on the other. "How did you come by this?" I have no idea where all these ideas have come from, but I do know that I picked the right lady that one night so long ago, at a dinner table on Tory. She really has been getting inside my head, in many more ways than one.

"Well, you have said all along that the subspecies have been responding to the Quarian domination and control, I simply stood up and took control. You were right, they are followers not leaders. We'll make them leaders."

Council members split off into groups continuing the discussion begun by Cor-ah ignoring Qadroth until the old man finally gave up and just slumped into his chair. He was done, but as with so many like him, was he really done? He and Riba were a serious threat to this new way of thinking, they had far too much to lose. The entire Quarian tribe had too much to lose. They have dominated all life in the universe for millions of years, it is inconceivable to think they would just roll over and play dead.

It was Rohn-Da that showed the political side of a Torrian mind. "As much as we may be hurt, our pride may have suffered at the hands of the Quarian, we must remember that they have led all these generations. They should not simply be turned out. They have much to offer and as we do, they have much to learn."

The discussions went on for what amounted to several days with members coming and going, meeting with leaders in their respective galaxies, returning to the table with new thoughts and ideas. Thinking was slowly replacing "follow the leader", and it made me think of what Thomas Jefferson and all his friends must have been going through when they created the United States of America. These men and women from hundreds of galaxies were acting individually and in concert on ideas of their own for the first time in history.

Cor-ah and Rohn-Da were the obvious leaders, and even little Tene, the Sarcathian who followed Qadroth like a puppy dog was joining in the debates. He was slow in mind but once he got hold of an idea, he manhandled it to completion. He made me think that his subspecies was in the first stages of their evolutionary move to being more like the humans. He was fully capable of learning but was also a bit lazy and could be corrupted. He'll end up being a successful politician on his world.

"Let's meet again in two weeks with new ideas, and hammer out this manuscript that we call a doctrine of order. This is the most important time in our history. We are doing something on our own without being coerced and controlled, without being threatened or dominated. Let's make damn sure we do it right." With that Cor-ah banged another meeting to a close to rounds of applause. Rohn-Da ended the first major council session leading to the downfall of the Quarian tribe by grabbing his eldest daughter in a huge hug. Chubby little Rohn-Da, the man I most wanted to bring to Earth with me after our first meeting was very close to being my new papa.

We were sitting at the kitchen table again, cups of mako in front of us when Cor-ah came up with a great idea. "Let's go to Earth. Let's go to Tom's home, listen to horrible noises, watch thousands of people doing things we've never heard of, and most importantly, I'm out of fudge." That brought all of us back to reality. "And, papa, you and Tom can share some ale. It is wonderful and I know you'll like it."

"As filled with joy as everyone is, I think we need to spend some time thinking about what the Quarian retaliation is going to be." That put a cold towel on the gathering for sure, but I needed to get this out. "They will not roll over and give up. And I've seen Riba when things didn't go exactly his way. This is a dangerous time for all of us.

"Rohn-Da, you probably know Riba better than anyone. What do you think we can expect from him and the rest of the Quarians?" In just a few days Rohn-Da has grown into a leader and he carries the mantle well. He is still the jolly little guy that's a bit pudgy, still has a grand sense of humor, but now has an aura that simply says, "I know what I'm doing." That is one of the first things one should look for in a leader. As I have come to expect, before he spoke, he looked first to Tanda, then to Cor-ah.

"I'm worried, too, Tom. Riba has always given the impression that he is aware of everything, knows what is going on everywhere, and is willing to force his will any time he feels it's necessary.   The Quarians aren't any stronger in their minds than any of the other subspecies but I think they have quailed the others into believing they are. That is their way of controlling us." He paused for just a moment, something I have seen all of the various subspecies do, recompartmentalizing their thoughts. "Riba is far more dangerous than Qadroth simply because he believes he is the supreme leader.   He believes and demands that we believe.   We must be cautious around him."

"I will never trust him again," Cor-ah said.   "It is interesting, though, that when I took control of the council there was no argument.   I've said it before and I believe it completely, my mind is stronger than his.   The one thing that he and other Quarians appear able to do, however, is pry into our thoughts without our knowledge.   If there is retaliation, this is how it will come about.   He and Qadroth and the other Quarians will know what we are doing and thinking most of the time.

"I don't know if we can stop that.   The other subspecies will be at the mercy of Riba and he can be mean.   You've said that right from the start you were afraid of him, Tom, and I know that right now I am, too."

Cor-ah, Tanda, Tetta, Rohn-Da and I sat quietly for a few minutes, our own thoughts taking shape, fear showing in all of our faces, maybe not fear, but anxiety for certain.   What was going to happen?   We have started a universe wide war.   There's a thought you don't hear often. Now the question is, can we pull it off without getting lots of people killed?

All I wanted to do was investigate some petroglyphs in the western desert of Nevada.   Such a simple thing, take some pictures, try to get an understanding of ancient people, and I'm in the middle of regime change on a universal scale.   I knew the minute I met Riba that he was dangerous, now I know just how dangerous that man is.

For the first time in, how long has it been? I don't have the immediate thought that I'm mad, that that lady in white with the cattle prod isn't about to attack. I'm terribly afraid of what might attack.

As dinner was being served in that special Torrian way, Riba showed up, and not in a party mood. He has become a vile little man with all of the attributes of one who relishes being in control and finds himself not in control. There were threats of violence, he actually started to take a step toward Rohn-Da when I moved between the two. Riba reacted quickly, was probably in the process of sending me back to Earth when Cor-ah slapped him across the side of the head with an open palm. I would imagine that slap could be heard hundreds of feet away, and Riba just stopped. Frozen in place. Cor-ah looked him in the eye, one dominant person looking at another dominant person, and Tanda immediately started crying.

Cor-ah never told us what she said to Riba, whether it was a threat or worse, but the little Aztec bowed slightly to her, wouldn't even look at me, and left the planet. "I'm terribly sorry you had to see that," she said, hugging me then her mother and sister, then her father. "The council has decided that elections for the central committee will be held next week. Riba will not be on the ballot and neither will Qadroth. There will be Quarians, but they will not be in the majority as we have discussed.

"Papa, I put your name on the ballot. After the committee is formed, then the permanent chairman will be determined from among the committee." She had gotten every bit of that knowledge from just a moment's look into Riba's mind and apparently said something to the little Aztec that actually frightened him. This woman is more and more the kind of person I've always wanted to know, and we've gone one step further. This is the kind of woman I've always wanted to love and have children with.

After dinner, as on that first night, Cor-ah and I went into the back yard and sat on that bench and watched the stars come out. "Of all those little pin pricks of light, one of them is the Marq system, the Milky Way? My home galaxy. Do you know which one it is?" I was thinking that it might be rather dominant but had no idea where to look. You know, creating a means of studying the universe and the history of the subspecies won't be that difficult, but my own studies of the ancient ones on Earth will probably not take place."

Cor-ah looked at me and I think she understood. "If you make contact with them, if they even slightly believe you might be from the future, you would be changing history. It's an ethical thing, isn't it?

"Tom, I've never even heard the word ethical before and I know what it means. How is that possible? Our minds are such that we feed on each other, don't we." It was a statement not a question.

"We have another task to take care of besides the council. As far as I can understand, the gatekeepers work at the behest of the Quarians. Is that right? Because if that is true, it will impede the flow of people between various times and spaces. Yannow would not respond to my marks in the sand when I was back on Earth the other day. He must have been told by Riba not to and that might prove to be difficult."

"The gatekeepers are supposed to work for the council, Tom. I may have to take a little jaunt to prove that point. I want you to come along because you know him better than I. Yannow likes you, I could tell that when we visited the cave. Let's do that in the morning. A quick visit to Earth, a ride in a vehicle, and a talk with Yannow. Right now, hot shot, it's bed time."

The problem with that is, we're in mama bear's house and we sleep alone. Even the leader of the Universal Council can't change that.

197

The visit to Earth was fast and furious. Tanda and Rohn-Da came with us and we spent just one day in Virginia City, seeing the sights before heading to Silver Peak and a visit with Yannow. Tanda was as frightened by the noise as Cor-ah had been but it didn't seem to affect Rohn-Da in the least. He and I went into the Bucket of Blood and had a couple of pints of beer, which he loved, and Cor-ah took Tanda for a visit along the main street and in particular the fudge shop. We had to make a mind jump to Silver Peak since there was no way for all of us to fit in the Jeep pick up.

"This is where I first met Riba," I said when we found ourselves outside the little cave along the edges of the Silver Peak Playa. "See these marks in the rocks here, those are petroglyphs and were made by people that lived and traveled through here thousands of years ago. That's what I was studying when Riba showed up and all of this got started."

We walked over to the cave and sat down in the shade. "Eight thousand years ago this cave was pretty large and deep and there was a waterfall flowing over the top there, creating a little stream that went into the lake that sat where that desert is now." I put the mark in the sand, not really expecting Yannow to appear, but I was wrong.

"There are problems in the universe Tom, but I'm glad to see you. The Universal Council is in turmoil, isn't it?"

"I'm afraid so, Yannow. You know Cor-ah and Rohn-Da, and this is Rohn-Da's wife, Tanda. The problem that Riba and Qadroth brought to me and to you, the idea of a nether world invasion, is not true. I think you know that now." He lowered his head a bit, scowling at the sandy floor of the cave, and agreed with me. "They wanted me to act as a patsy, my friend, but humans just aren't that way. We're here right now to make sure that the gate keepers will continue working for the Universal Council, not any particular galaxy or subspecies."

He was looking directly at me and was about to speak when Cor-ah spoke first. "We are building a new Universal Council, Yannow, one in which all the various subspecies will have an equal voice. One in which there is no domination by any one group. It is very important to the continued fellowship of the council that the gates through which time can be traveled remain open. One thing that has been missing for thousands of generations is knowledge of the history of the universe, of how and why things take place today, of who past leaders may have been.

"The gate keepers can play a very large part in bringing the universe back into good order in which all of us can live in peace and in knowledge. We need you very much."

Yannow, this magnificent Yeti, stands well over seven feet tall, is as imposing as anything one could imagine, and his voice was as soft and comforting as any I have ever heard as he spoke. "The gate keepers have always worked for the council, Cor-ah, and that will not change. Riba has attempted to make us a tool of the Quarians, but it isn't working. We are very special in the scheme of things in this universe, we know history as no other group could, even you, Tom, and we as a tribe have already reached a conclusion on the matter. We will work with the Universal Council as we always have and will maintain these portals at all times."

He said, "We know history as no other group could." He just answered the major question that has made this tale impossible to fathom. An entire universe that has no understanding of history, has no desire to learn, and all because of the arrogance of the Quarians. If I go back in time with Yannow, I'll bet that there was a time when history was very important, that it was taught, that the concept of understanding on the one hand and wanting to learn on the other a way of life.

"Yannow, it will be just a short time, in your calculations that the council will be back in full operation, and there are things that must be done. There must be an education system in each of the galaxies, there must be a known history of the universe, and there must be opportunity for people to learn and prosper. It appears that I am among the very few that even know what the word history means, and yet the knowledge of the past must be rich. Can we work together on this?"

Yannow took a long deep breath into that mighty chest and slowly gave me a lesson. "I understood what you were saying before you said it, Tom. Yes, it wasn't that many thousands of years ago that history, education, knowledge was a big part of life in the universe. Only the Earth people maintained the ideas that were brought forward by my tribes. Only the Quarians detested the entire concept. To bring that back to the rest of the subspecies would be the most wonderful thing I can think of. Yes, Tom, between you and the rest of my tribe, history will live again.

"Cor-ah, Rohn-Da, do you know why your homes are cylindrical while those on Earth are squared?"

When I had asked that question, there had been blank stares. Now, Cor-ah poked me in the ribs, a little harder than necessary, and said, "no." Yannow chuckled, and said it had started as a Quarian's very mean joke, and that there was no real reason.

He was actually smiling as he said this and wanted to know if there was anything else he could do for us.

"I think we need to go home," I said.

Yannow actually snickered a little bit and said, "Tom, which home?" Everyone said "Torry" at the same time.

The next several weeks were filled with hassle, excitement, danger, and warmth, all wrapped around major meetings of the council, major confrontations with various members of the Quarian tribes, and most of all, anxiety over what Riba and Qadroth might yet bring as their counter attack.

"Rohn-Da, have there ever been times when physical violence was a way of defeating someone? On Earth, it is very prevalent, but I haven't heard anyone here mention beatings or murder or physical attacks. Is it something we should worry about?"

The whole family sat in contemplation for a moment and it was Cor-ah that spoke rather than Rohn-Da. "I've never heard of anyone actually hurting someone by way of physical violence, but there is another way that Quarians threaten people. As you know, Riba has the strength to simply transport you to another place. Imagine if you were unable to counter that strength. Whether Quarians have actually sent people to horrible places or not, the threat has always been there."

If I hadn't been all but a member of this family, I doubt that anyone would have passed that information on to me. Every set of eyes were downcast, lips were quivering, thoughts were being passed about. This amounted to unlocking a deep family secret, one that was obviously not to be discussed. Cor-ah took my hand, gently squeezed it, and gave me a deep look, deeper than I've ever seen from her. "This, then, might be the means of retaliation and we must come up with a way to counteract that possibility. Is that why you walked right up and smacked Riba? Is that how you were able to keep him from sending me off somewhere?" What a brave thing to do, to slap your adversary across the face knowing you could be banished somewhere. On Earth, an open handed slap in the face is an open invitation to a huge brawl. It is also a very good way to stop a fool from carrying on. Cor-ah used the open handed slap to simply put Riba in his place, to tell him he was no longer the boss.

Cor-ah must be the strongest willed person I've ever met in my life. Do I have enough in me to do the same if she was threatened like that? I hope I never have to find out. She screwed up her face with half a smile and half a scowl, giggled just enough to break the tension.

"I've wanted to do that so many times, Tom, you will never know. That arrogant little bastard has played with this family, teased mama into tears, threatened papa, and even mimicked Tetta. We always gave in to him because of the implied threats of being banished somewhere.

"After watching Qadroth collapse at the meeting that day, I'm not sure now that they could actually send another subspecies somewhere they didn't want to go, but I don't think anyone has ever tried. He could send you, Tom, because humans have not had our abilities for years. You wouldn't have any idea of how to transport yourself somewhere. How would you know how to stop from being transported? I think this is an implied weapon, one they might threaten us with, but not be able to actually use."

I'm still intrigued about this ability to move about, through time and space, from galaxy to galaxy, using just a mind. Why have those from Earth lost that ability? Quarians are telling us that they took that ability away from us, but I'm getting back to the idea that it is simply a case of genetic evolution changing the abilities of humans. What will be most interesting will be to find out when, in relation for instance to the time of the first humans. That could be a way to judge when some of the other subspecies will find future generations becoming less and less able to have the mind strength they have today.

This will be a big move forward in the history of the universe. Cor-ah will have to work very closely with me, and I'm going to be working very closely with Yannow. I can't, I don't dare interfere with the old people on Earth for purely ethical reasons, but the history of the universe wouldn't create that type of problem. Cor-ah was giving me the evil eye again.

Her mind was complex, not like other Torrians or other subspecies except for Quarians and humans and she learned how to use those complexities by being around me. That means that I will be able to develop a teaching program for the other galaxies.

"Yes, I think you will." She was smiling broadly and knew that I was still planning to be part of this family. "When I slapped Riba I broke his concentration and he was unable to send you back to Earth. But more than that, I think. If he really had the power to send me somewhere that look I got from him convinced me he would have. They know they can't do that, but they continue to use the threat as a weapon to continue their control over us.

"I'm going to take a little jaunt now, and anyone is welcome to come with me. I'm going to prove this point. Who wants to go?" My hand was first up, then Tanda's, then Tetta's, and my pudgy little papa in law finally put his up. With that, we were up on that little hillside calling for a gatekeeper.

"If I'm right, and Yannow said he thought this was going to happen, the Quarians have attempted to coerce the gatekeepers into only reacting to a Quarian signal. Yannow told us that, but there are still ways that he could keep control. Let's see." We all sat in a semi-circle while Cor-ah made the sign in the dirt with her finger tip, and there he was, Yeti in full bloom, sitting in the dirt right alongside us.

"Human Tom. Riba said I wasn't to respond to your calls, that humans have been banished from the universal family. I must leave now."

"Wait. It wasn't Tom that called, it was I and you know you must respond to a Torrian or any other subspecies. I need to talk with you for a few minutes, because there have been some major changes in the universal council that affect you as much as it does us. We left Yannow not too long ago and he, too, is spreading the word. It just hasn't reached you yet. It will."

"Very well, Cor-ah, but Riba will not be pleased that human Tom is here."

"That, of course, is Riba's problem, my friend." She spent about ten minutes bringing the gate keeper up to speed, and he promised to spread the word among the various tribes. He was amazed at how he and the other gate keepers had been manipulated for so many centuries.

"That must be why Yannow has called for a full meeting of the tribe. You talked with him and he is our leader." He got contemplative, sat in the dirt next to us, stroked that well bearded chin, and slowly started talking.

"This is part of why humans have not been able to be with us. I've never fully understood, but now I do. Humans and Quarians are simply too much alike to exist in the same areas." This great hulk of Yeti was laughing out loud, thumping the ground with his massive fists, coming very close to knocking Tanda and Tetta on their backs, and taking great pleasure in his thoughts. "To answer your other question, as far as I know, there is no special power or strength that Quarians have that would allow them to banish someone with the abilities of the members of a subspecies other than human. They might threaten, but it couldn't be done."

"I have a question." He looked at me with a different glint in his eye. He had contemplated not allowing us to talk to him because of me, now he is looking like he wants to know something from us. That's a good thing. "The universal council is made up of members of subspecies from all the various galaxies in the universe, and you and your tribes exist in all of those galaxies, even including the Marq system where I'm from. Why aren't there members of the gate keepers sitting at counsel? You have a large job, you have knowledge and capabilities few others have, your presence would be beneficial, I would think."

Rohn-Da answered the question, and it wasn't a good answer. "The gate keepers are not considered members of the various subspecies, Tom. Riba and Qadroth would not let them sit as members of the council." So, the Quarians also have the same racial prejudices as humans, or is it the other way around? Once again, I'm a bit humiliated at being a human with too many Quarian genes surging through my system.

"I think we can change that when the new council and new orders take effect. There are many problems that will need to be addressed as soon as possible. Thank you for making us clear on this, my old friend. I'll let you know when the next council meeting is going to be held. I would like representatives from the gate keepers to be present." Rohn-Da just made one huge decision on behalf of the entire universe. We all shook hands, and within moments were back in the family kitchen.

"Papa, mama, I think Tom and I need to get away for a couple of days. I think we are going to go back to Earth for a short time. You know how to let me know if we need to return." She looked at me really hard, and laid it out plainly. "I have a legal paper that Tom needs to fulfill. I'm out of fudge."

The laughter was still echoing in my mind as we found ourselves in my kitchen in Virginia City, dressed as humans would dress, western shirts, jeans, and boots. Amazing.

Chapter Fifteen

"We can talk here, Tom, and I am afraid even here, that Riba or Qadroth or one of the other Quarians will be listening to what we have to say. I'm sure that Yannow is right in that Quarians cannot actually send someone away, banish them to a horrible end, but with you, we both know it can happen. I can't send you away, but I can bring you with me. What special powers they have, I don't have, and this is really beginning to bother me." I had a cup of mako on the table in front of me that fast. She brought some with her, and I wonder if there was any roqua to nibble on.

"No. Now quit, this is important." The little frown was a front, I knew that, she was setting me up for something. "I won't be protecting myself tonight, Tom. I won't. If Riba or Qadroth beat us at this game, I will have part of you." She was as close to crying as I have ever seen her. It was cuddle time, and even that didn't happen.

Qadroth was standing in the middle of my living room, dressed as a Quarian, not as a human, which caught my attention immediately. He was back into his regal self, elegant, eloquent, silver hair all in place. "I'm not an evil man, Tom, I want you to believe that." He was uncomfortable as hell, and there was something else that I simply couldn't put a handle on. There was some reason for him to be here, and he may not have been totally aware of the entire picture. Was he sent by Riba? I couldn't get a hint of anything from Cor-ah's attitude either.

"Cor-ah, I said some very nasty things to you and about you and I apologize. I was wrong, very wrong, and I know that now. I'm here against the wishes of Riba, he may or may not know I'm here, but I wanted to warn you, Tom, he wants you dead. I can't stop him. This is as much as I can do." Qadroth was tired, in his eyes, in his slouch, even his demeanor looked tired and I asked him to sit with us, have a cup of mako. He offered a gentle smile and asked if he could talk, just between us. This is not the Qadroth I have seen at council and I said, "yes" immediately.

"Riba is more than just a Quarian, Tom, he is descended from the original tribe, isn't of this time as you know it. We, that is, you, me, Cor-ah, are in the present time right now, but Riba, he's from a different time, long, long ago. He has a power of manipulation that others of the species don't have, dating back to the beginning of the tribe. Riba is not one of us. For generations he has taken control of the universal council by intimidating people like me. I'm afraid, Tom, Cor-ah, that you have been dealing with a fake. I'm not the chairman, Riba is and in his mind, always will be."

"I'm hoping that has ended," Cor-ah said. "But tell me about this intimidation. I know Quarians have used intimidation to get their way, threatening to send someone to a horrible place or banishment, or some such, but Yannow, the gate keeper, says Quarians don't have that ability. Tell me about Riba."

"I could not send you or Tom or anyone else anywhere he didn't want to go. As you, Cor-ah, I can bring someone along with me, but I, or any other Quarian cannot send someone without their consent. Riba on the other hand may be able to do that. No one has ever pushed him far enough to really find out, but the threat has been used many times.

"As I said, Riba is not of this time and may have powers none of us have." He got contemplative for a minute, compartmentalizing all his thoughts, unlike the unkempt mind of a human, and continued. "You were trying to tell us about what will be happening over the next many generations, Tom, and I think I understood most of it. You were right, though, about understanding our history. It has been kept from the subspecies in order for Quarians to have control, power, the ability to make all the decisions.

"The gate keepers have kept a history, something they teach their young, and have mentioned to me more than once that it is wrong not to know what has happened in the past.

"This is why Riba is very dangerous right now. For him to survive, he must maintain control otherwise there is no reason for him to exist. He will do what he is capable of to keep that control, and that means that you and Cor-ah are in great danger. I must go, because Riba probably knows I've been here and will be very angry.

"As I said, both of you, I'm sorry for my conduct. I'm glad you figured everything out, Tom. I'm glad the lies and deception are over with, finally. Cor-ah the new universal council is indeed universal, and you must be congratulated on that." In a moment, he was gone.

"Riba is a very dangerous person, Tom," Cor-ah said, "and if Qadroth knows where we are, then so does Riba. I didn't think I would ever hear a Quarian say the things Qadroth just said. So, my human friend, lover, and soon-to-be papa, you have created one hell of a mess, what do you plan to do about that?" That little smile was playing about the edges of her mouth, her eyes were dancing with humor, and I was on the hot seat one more time.

"How do you do that? Turn it into my problem instead of ours or just yours? Well, whatever happens, it is our problem and you are right that Riba must know where we are right now. You want to fill me in on that soon-to-be papa bit?" All I got in answer was a Cor-ah smile and a peck on the cheek. If keeping one's lover in the dark is game with Torrian women, Cor-ah is a master.

"I'm asking Mom and Dad to join us, and with all of us here, Riba will have to be as cautious as he has ever been.   That is, underhanded, devious, criminal.   I'm worried, but I know with all of us here he will have to be

208

very careful." She got up and walked to the window, looked down on C Street, and gave just a little crack of a smile. "Fudge, my friend, fudge."

As I got up from the couch, Riba appeared, almost exactly where Qadroth had been standing, looking like a combination of the world's worst thunderstorm mixed with a full-fledged tsunami. "You two will go to council tomorrow and tell the council you have been lying, that the nether people are invading this universe, that they must be stopped. Cor-ah, you will relinquish everything you have taken from the Quarian tribes, and you will be banished to Torry, never to be allowed to leave. Tom Henry, you will never be allowed to leave Earth under any circumstances after your last meeting with the council." His eyes were cold, almost white, they were so gray, and his skin was every color, as I had seen in council before.

Riba was no longer the little Aztec that I met in the Nevada desert so long ago. He was a threat, a danger, and an enemy. "You can't banish Cor-ah, old one. She is the interim chairperson of the universal council. You can't even send her away or have any effect on her. She is Torrian, Riba, and she will win this fight. There is no nether invasion and you knew that when you lied to me to get me to help you with whatever your scheme has been. You picked the wrong subspecies to do your dirty work." He was planted in the middle of my living room, glaring, first at me, then at Cor-ah, and if evil could talk, he was screaming.

I looked over at Cor-ah, and there was just the hint of that smile moving about on her face, almost a gaze at Riba, and she spoke slow, not tense, and with amazing human thinking. "The Quarian tribes are welcome to be members of the universal council for all time, Riba, but there will no longer be special privileges for you. Those days have ended. You will no longer be allowed to force your will on subspecies or on individuals as you are trying to do with Tom. These aren't my orders, Riba, they come straight from the council and all Quarians will be made aware soon. Do not threaten me, Tom, or any member of the council again." She wanted to slug the mean little guy, but, of course, didn't. He wanted to slug her and, thankfully didn't, because he would have died on the spot.

"Riba, tell me, exactly what period of time is it that you have come from? You're not from this period, I know that. You have spent generations manipulating the Quarians and the rest of the subspecies in order to get your own way, but how long have you been doing this?" He wasn't expecting this and almost gave me a straight answer. He stammered, glowered at me, and shut his mouth immediately.

"Old man, how did you come up with the idea of an invasion from an opposite universe? It almost worked, you know. It was that one little wild Quarian gene that started acting up, first in humans, then in Torrians, but I wonder, Riba, did it also start acting up in Quarians, and that's why an answer had to be created?" Riba was defeated but would never admit to it. Cor-ah must have sensed something because in a blink we were at the little cave outside Silver Peak, and it was eight thousand years before my birth.

I wonder if maybe this is Riba's actual time. He keeps coming back to this time, like it's a home place, comfortable and possibly filled with energy that he can draw upon. Riba is more than just an ancient Quarian, I think, he's someone slightly outside the species. The eight thousand years before my birth time must be his real time.

I'm sure Riba did not intend on having Cor-ah along on this little trip into the past. This would have been my last ride through time and space if she hadn't been so smart, so fast at thinking, and joined us. The old guy was furious when he saw all three of us standing just inside the cave with water pouring down outside the entrance.

"Didn't expect me, eh Riba?   You cannot harm me or anyone else and you know it.   And you are not going to harm Tom."

Without benefit of making the signs in the sand, Yannow appeared immediately, standing alongside the three of us.   "I didn't call you, Yannow.   You aren't needed here," Riba said, anger boiling to the surface.   "Gate keepers do not appear without being called, Yannow. Leave now."   Imperial in his pantaloons and boots, and only two or so feet shorter than the Yeti, the Quarian didn't stand a chance.

"We serve the council, Riba.   Cor-ah is the chairman of the council and asked that I join you.   I'm afraid your days of ordering us around have ended.   The gate keeper tribes have just completed a meeting in which the offers made by the council have been accepted."   He looked over at Cor-ah, and once again, I have seen a Yeti smile.   "Thank you, Cor-ah for allowing us to have full membership on the council, it will be a sincere pleasure to serve with you."   Then he looked at Riba and for the first time ever, I believe I saw fear in the old man's eyes.

"If you try to harm Human Tom in any way, you will have to go through me to accomplish that task.   As gate keeper, it is I who says who goes where and to what time they go.   Riba, it may be time for you to return to your own time because there are new ways coming to the universe, ways in which you will no longer have control over those that bring the change."   Now, I have found out, a Yeti can also be quite philosophical.   Amazing. We may not be in Riba's original time.   He may even be older than this.

Cor-ah gave a quick scream, I felt things mixing up inside me, and Yannow gave a mighty roar that bounced off every rock in the cave.   I found myself on my back under the waterfall with a huge Yeti all but sitting on me and a very dead Quarian spread face down in the water.

Cor-ah rushed under the falls and grabbed me, actually pulling me out from under Yannow and dragged me into the cave. Yannow got up slowly and came inside, sitting in the sand next to me, and Cor-ah created a little fire near us.

As we watched, Riba's body slowly faded from view. "He is now in his own time, Tom." Yannow looked horrible, and fear was still written in Cor-ah's face. "For the first time in generations, the universe is free from his grasping control and manipulation."

"What the hell happened?" I didn't have a clue other than Riba was dead and it looked like Yannow killed him. Cor-ah for all her strength was crying very softly, and I saw something I couldn't believe. Yannow reached his long heavily muscled arm out and drew her in, holding her close. He had tears running down broad cheeks as well, and I'm positive I did, too.

"I've never killed anyone before. This is very strange because I don't feel any regret at all." Yannow was speaking as softly as a Yeti can, staring down into the flames, little muscle spasms shaking his huge frame, hugging my woman. "Riba has always been an evil man, Tom. Evil."

"Is he really Quarian?" I had another thought dancing around that Riba was from a species before the Quarian tribes came in existence, maybe with powers far greater than the Quarians of today, and that evolution was already at work on the current breed known as Quarian.

"That may be, Tom. I want you to spend a great deal of time with my people as soon as calm is restored. We have a history of the universe, written, catalogued, bound, and protected that you will find to serve you as you rebuild an educated universe. At some point, as you have made clear, the genes that altered the humans will alter all the subspecies, even the Quarians, and the knowledge of the past will be a necessity.

"You know that more than anyone. You may not be able to include the humans in this because they have not had contact with other galaxies for thousands of generations. Humans here in the Marq system have been outsiders for so long it will be impossible to include them."

"I will contact you as soon as I have an idea of how to go about all of this, Yannow. There are no words strong enough or filled with enough love to thank you for saving my life. We will have a long and wonderful relationship, my friend. And teaching apparently is what I'm here for."

Cor-ah gave Yannow a kiss on the brow and I found myself sitting at my kitchen table back in Virginia City with a cup of mako at hand. Before anything could be said, Tanda, Rohn-Da, and Tetta were also sitting at my table, with Cor-ah standing behind me. "This way, Tom, I only have to tell the story once," and she sat down, too.

Cor-ah brought everyone up to date right up to the point where something really bad happened at the cave. For the first time, I was aware that either Tanda or Rohn-Da had discussed the differences between Tetta and her family and she apparently understood fully. As near as I could tell, this entire conversation would be verbal, not by the powerful minds of this family.

"Tom, we're going to have to devise a way of talking that these others won't understand, like they do to us," and she laughed right out loud. "That would be fun." Tetta, like her entire family had a wonderful sense of humor. It's a shame Quarians don't. In all the time I knew Riba, I saw him smile once, and I'm wondering if that wasn't forced.

Cora was looking me right in the face, saying, "When Riba started to send you off somewhere that I couldn't pick up on, Yannow apparently could. I have never been that frightened, it seems like I say that a lot when I'm around you, dear husband, but it's true. Yannow reached out grabbed Riba by the throat and whipped him like a rope. I actually heard his neck snap, but you were almost on your way, Tom.

"When Riba died, you fell into the creek under the waterfall and Yannow tripped when he threw Riba outside the cave and fell on top of you. I was terrified, screaming your name, and then I saw you guys were okay. Yannow saved your life Tom, he really did."

Everyone was settled at the table and I was, once again, completely befuddled. "Okay pretty lady, give it up. You said earlier today 'soon-to-be papa' and just a minute ago said, 'dear husband'. What is going on? Rohn-Da's and Tanda's eyes were focused on the table top, Tetta was in a giggle farm, and Cor-ah had that look I have called 'I Win'. "Tell me." Of course, a human threatening a Torrian isn't going to work, and Cor-ah simply got up and walked up behind me again.

"I'm pregnant with twins, Tom, so you are 'soon-to-be papa'. And, since I feel it is only right that we be married if we're going to be a family, I have announced our marriage. That's so simple, and you don't understand." She just eased her way over to the counter, and actually physically made a pot of coffee for all of us. I sat at the table, me, married, papa Tom, grinning like a fool.

The talk went on for hours of course, but finally I said it was time for Rohn-Da and I to go have a cold beer. Cor-ah took Tanda and Tetta in hand and headed for the fudge shop after warning them of the terrible noises and things they would see.

Chapter Sixteen

"Limited knowledge given to a limited number of people coupled with management by intimidation. That's how Riba maintained his handle on all these billions of people, Rohn-Da." We were on our second bottle of good old American ale when the full impact of the situation grabbed me and I almost burst out in uncontrolled laughter. My happy little, now papa-in-law, Torrian friend didn't pick up on the irony.

"Rohn-Da, you are probably the first inter-galactic visitor to ever down a cold one at the Bucket of Blood saloon, and if I introduced you that way there wouldn't be a soul in here to believe me. This is what Yannow meant when he said my teaching would have to be everywhere except Earth. And, ironically again, it is Earth that is responsible for this major revolution among the subspecies in the universe."

We stood at the long oaken bar with an ancient mirror behind it, two hundred year old Victorian lamps hanging from the ceiling, talking about a subject that started millions of years ago. There is no way I could ever broach this subject with another human being. "Rohn-Da, I'm going to have to do my work from Torry. How could I do it from here? I certainly can't bring Yannow in for a cold beer, now can I?"

We were both laughing, actually out loud over that. "Yannow would empty this place in half a second, Tom," and he had a real Torrian belly laugh. "That bartender would be out the door first." He calmed down a bit, gave me one of his special Torrian hugs, which one rarely sees between men on Earth, and we finished our beer.

"Riba must have sensed the genetic changes that were taking place among the Quarians back in his time. The Quarians must have been extraordinarily strong then,

215

and with a devious mind worked up with fears of losing control, he started working toward the continuing dominance of his species. Qadroth was just the last in a long line of dupes, Rohn-Da. Riba probably had a hand in having the humans removed from the council hundreds of thousands of years ago to not let any Quarians or other subspecies have an idea of the genetic evolution taking place.

"And, that's why there is no knowledge of a universal council or an ability to travel through time and space among humans today. The removal was so far back in human history, well before any recorded history, that the happening simply went away. There are some six billion people on Earth right now, Rohn-Da, and four Torrians, and one human and four Torrians know what the hell I'm talking about."

As we walked out the swinging doors of the old saloon, a couple of motorcycles went by. "What the hell are those, Tom?" He was startled, and inquisitive at the same time.

"Motorcycles, Rohn-Da. Two wheeled vehicles, instead of four wheels."

"We'll have to work on getting a couple of those to Torry," he said and we climbed the stairs to my apartment. The girls were munching on fudge, and Tanda and Tetta were both talking at the same time about what they had seen and heard. Rohn-Da immediately told them about motorcycles. Chaos was rampant at my kitchen table.

It appears we'll have dinner on Torry tonight.

-end-

About the author

I've had a wonderful and varied time along this bumpy highway called life. I spent my early years in Santa Cruz, California, swimming, fishing, and wallowing in the splendor of redwoods, the Monterey Bay, and a loving family. Then, my four years of high school were spent living on the Island of Guam. That was back in the early 1950s Yes, Virginia, I am that old, but only in body, not spirit.

My first job in radio was in 1958. I bought the Virginia City Legend newspaper in that old western mining community in 1971, and retired from having a job in 2010. That's when I changed from being a reporter of news to being a writer of fiction, and over these last few years have found my western and crime/mystery short stories published in magazines and anthologies, around the world.

My beautiful wife Patty and I live on a small hobby farm about twenty miles north of Reno, Nevada, sharing space with a couple of fine horses, a flock of egg-producing chickens, and some breeding rabbits. You're always welcome to visit. I need help cleaning those corrals.

If you enjoyed this book, you may also like:

Hegira
By: Jim Cronin

His species became extinct decades before the aliens rescued and cloned him, but he still must do everything he can to save them all. Karm must travel back in time, create the most powerful financial empire ever seen on the planet Dyan'ta and assemble a team of experts who must be kept in the dark about his plans for fear of upsetting the timeline.

Dr. Jontar Rocker is an up and coming geneticist whose untested and controversial theories on cloning become the lynch pin in Karm's schemes. Maripa, Karm's petite and beautiful surrogate niece, personal secretary, and deadly bodyguard must learn to trust Karm despite his deceptions and secrets. Can the emerging love between Dr. Rocker and Maripa survive the demons and surprises of their own past, as well as Karm's impenetrable air of mystery?

Karm and his companions must save the Brin. To do so, they must band together to overcome Brach, the ambitious and obsessed monarch. Determined to take control of Karm's vast industrial empire, Brach joins forces with his conniving brother Pareth, leader of The Faith an ultra-conservative religious order committed to stopping Dr. Rocker and his heretical efforts to develop cloning techniques. Nothing less than survival of their species is at stake.

For more titles, visit us online:
www.solsticepublishing.com

www.ingramcontent.com/pod-product-compliance
Lightning Source LLC
Chambersburg PA
CBHW051131020726
47501CB00005B/1460